THE VENOMOUS SERPENT

The brass in the Derbyshire village church depicts Sir Humphrey and Sybil de Latours. Strangely, despite the clear detail elsewhere, the face of Sybil is obliterated. However, Sally Fenton takes a rubbing to hang in the bedroom. But at night, in the moonlight, static objects begin to move — and writhe. The rubbing takes on a life of its own. Soon life in the village becomes a nightmare, and Sally and her partner are powerless to stop the evil spreading . . .

Books by Brian Ball
in the Linford Mystery Library:

DEATH OF A LOW HANDICAP MAN
MONTENEGRIN GOLD

BRIAN BALL

THE VENOMOUS SERPENT

Complete and Unabridged

LINFORD
Leicester

First published in Great Britain

First Linford Edition
published 2008

British Library CIP Data

Ball, Brian, *1932* –
   The venomous serpent.—Large print ed.—
Linford mystery library
1. Horror tales
2. Large type books
I. Title
823.9'14 [F]

ISBN 978–1–84782–408–0

Published by
F. A. Thorpe (Publishing)
Anstey, Leicestershire

Set by Words & Graphics Ltd.
Anstey, Leicestershire
Printed and bound in Great Britain by
T. J. International Ltd., Padstow, Cornwall

This book is printed on acid-free paper

1

Thin moonlight streaked the high white tower. Then black rain slashed and its massive bulk was hidden. A growl of thunder told the hurrying men that the storm was gathering; though their cloaks were sodden through and through they did not welcome the thought of the shelter ahead. Tonight the church was no sanctuary.

The priest at the head of the small procession waved his lantern in encouragement, then lost his footing in the mud. A watcher might have thought the sight comical, for he was a tall, thin, ungainly man with the unsteady gait of a heron. He picked himself up from the slimy mud, careful to keep the lantern upright and more careful yet to keep the wafer in his left hand dry. It might have brought a smile to the face of a watcher but for the ghastly white of his face and the strained, haunted look in his eyes.

One look at his countenance would have stilled a ribald comment, dismissed a smile; for, like the men who followed, he was afraid. More, he was in a state of terror. He was engaged in an undertaking that was beyond his understanding. That night, forces that must forever be a mystery to him would assemble. He sweated with terror. In the archaic phrase of his day, he was afraid unto death.

Behind him a man groaned aloud in a torment. The priest turned, his voice a shriek above the wind's howling:

'No turning back, masters! See, we are in the care of Holy Church! I have the blessed wafer and the water both! No harm can befall us, if we but keep our hearts!'

Nevertheless, one of the men stumbled as the priest had done before. The hurdle swayed, and the shrouded still form might have fallen off the rough platform.

'Have a care!' growled a burly, thickset man. 'Our work is yet to be done — if once the moonlight falls on the Beast, the foul thing is loose again!'

He balanced the massive wooden

hurdle against his thigh until the bearer was on his feet again. The man sobbed in fright, but he took comfort from the resolution of the thickset man.

The priest raised his lantern,

'All is well, Master Priest!' the thickset man said. 'Lead on, and let us be done with this foul thing!'

The men looked at the priest's face and found no comfort. There was true dedication and real religious fervour in it, but he was terrified, just as they were. They saw his soft hands and remembered his high-pitched voice The men of the parish had taken matters into their own hands: the priest would officiate, as was his duty, but they would make sure that the brutal and hideous thing that had to be done was carried through by their own hard, powerful hands. Butcher's work needed their strength.

When they reached the new church porch, they had recovered something of their earlier determination. The hurdle they carried was heavy, but there were enough of them to make the burden light for each man there: what lay on it added little to the beams and wet planks. The wife of the Lord of Stymead had not been a large woman. And this thing she called her lapdog was little larger than the cub of a hound. Both lay wrapped in the grave-windings.

It was the priest who was near the end of his strength. Terror, stark soul-ripping terror, had drained him. Perhaps because he had more knowledge of the thing they faced he was enfeebled almost to the point of exhaustion. Yet something sustained him when they reached the porch.

'Put fear aside,' he said, in his natural voice. He swung back the oaken doors and gestured to the men. 'All is ready.'

He lit a dozen lamps. The bearers had not put down the hurdle. They stood before the chancel staring down into the gaping pit.

'Mine is the worst part,' said the burly man. 'But all must do theirs. So let us be done!'

The priest looked at the men of the Parish as they handled the tools of their various trades. There were masons, a smith, a carpenter; and a butcher. His face showed revulsion as the burly man fingered the edge of a heavy chopping-knife. Now that he was in his own church, the priest felt more assured. He could busy himself in the preparations for the lengthy rituals that were indicated in the sacred books. In his dripping robes, he moved with more confidence now; much of the terror that had been with him since the villagers had taken him to the night-creature and its frightful familiar had been dissipated.

He no longer thought of what lay within the shroud.

'God be with us this night, and all His angels, my masters,' he called when all was ready. 'We have need of all His Grace and Powers to preserve us from the Enemy of Mankind.'

He shuddered as the men knelt before the altar. A memory of their shocked and bewildered faces came back to him. They had found the evil creatures by chance. Too drugged to stir from the spot, the creatures of night had been easily captured and enshrouded. But what when they should wake! He gabbled his words in fresh fear:

'The Almighty has this night delivered unto us the foul pests that have haunted our village for the past year. You have discovered the lair of the venomous serpent, yet it is right that the Lady of Stymead should lie beside her husband, the gallant knight Lord Humphrey de Latours, when the foul spirit that holds her soul in thrall has been duly exorcised!'

He would have said more, had not the burly man interrupted:

'Exorcise away, priest! I would be home before dawn's light.'

The others murmured in agreement. More than one looked to the dripping hurdle and its still burden.

'So be it,' said the priest. He looked again to the knife in the burly man's grip. With it, the swine-killer could sever the head of a boar at one stroke. 'Strike for the evil heart, then truly cut off her head!'

'I am ready, priest.'

The thunder crashed out at that moment, a heavy and sullen roaring that shook the beams of the high chancel. Crisp, blue-white light flared through the narrow windows as lightning played in a vast sheet across one entire side of the horizon, bathing the church and the village beyond in a ghastly glow. Huge thunder-peals followed, leaving the assembled men stunned and reeling from the effect of the successive shocks. Some called out to God and the saints. Others rushed to the porch, only to run back in helpless terror as more thunder-claps roared over the church. And still the lightning bathed the chancel and the narrow, sinister pit in a wash of corpse-light.

The priest gathered his wits.

'Fear nothing, men of Stymead!' he cried, his voice shaking. 'It is a trick of the Adversary. It is a show to seize your hearts and allow the venomous serpent to be free! You are safe in this house — come forward and hear the words of the Holy Book! Listen to the words that will send this evil into the Pit from which it came!'

Several turned and knelt again before the altar. But the swine-killer's nerve had failed. The heavy knife slipped from his grasp, to fall with a ringing clatter on the flagstones. As it jangled into silence, the priest intoned the prayers that would contain the undead things that had plagued the village so foully.

He broke the wafer and sprinkled holy water. He took the nail that was assuredly from the Cross itself; it would pin the brass plate in place and keep the night-creatures within if all else failed. All was ready.

'Courage!' he called, and he was stronger than at any time that night, for the words of the ritual had comforted him. 'Take off the shroud — it is time!'

Not one of the men moved. He tried again, for all was ready. Mortar had been mixed. A coffin lay open. Lead sheeting gleamed in the yellow light. But the thunder had unmanned the parishioners. Its terrible pounding, and the accompanying blue-white lightning, had confirmed their belief that the Devil himself was striding across the night to keep one of his creatures from their vengeance. In vain the priest pleaded. He spoke of the nightly visitations of the things that lay within the grave-windings, of good men lost and children savaged, but it was to no avail. Even as he argued, the priest thought he saw a shadow of movement where one white, icy hand lay hidden.

Lightning bathed the hurdle again, and a pale, watery gleam of sustained light picked out the stones, the alabaster blocks and the bright engraving.

The priest trembled. 'Moonlight!' he groaned. He summoned all his resolution and shrilled to the palsied men: 'Since you fear to look on her face, see how a priest of God can do your work for you! Be forever ashamed, men of Stymead!'

Saying this, he picked up the broad-bladed knife and sliced into the sodden linen of the shroud. Too wet to give easily, it resisted his unskilled efforts. But he cut, and cut, and the windings parted. Slight whimpering noises came from the hypno-tised men around him.

'Leave be, priest!' implored someone. 'Leave be the terrible thing, in God's Name!'

'In God's Name I shall destroy the venomous serpent!' he shrilled.

And then the form was revealed.

All had seen it but the priest. He had been summoned on this night when the creature and its frightful familiar had been tracked to its lair; but by the time he arrived, the hurdle was ready and the body enshrouded. Now, he saw the ivory skin, the deep black hair, the vile red lips, the half-smile, the fangs, the taloned fingers the sensuous, evil curves of the beautifully-formed body all for the first time; and the small, sleeping thing at the feet of what had been the Lady Sybil de Latours. He might have been fascinated, or revulsed, or stupefied, for it was also the first time he had seen a beautiful, naked female body.

One white, taloned hand moved.

The priest shrieked high and long, an animal noise like that of a dying night thing. His parishioners echoed the yell. Thunderclaps roared back, and the eyelids of the sleeping, sated woman-thing began to flicker.

The priest let the knife slip, just as had the swine-butcher. It jangled once again. And then the priest fell to the ground.

The sound of metal on stone brought some of the men from their helpless swooning fright. A small man crept forward in spite of the stirrings of the dreadful creature on the hurdle.

Thomas, too, recovered. He growled, anger in his voice:

'How is the priest?'

'Dead — stark dead!'

More men growled fiercely into their heavy beards.

'In God's own House!'

'A man of little account, but a good priest nevertheless!' Thomas called. 'And dead by the touch of the Beast!'

It was so, for a mark glowed on the dead cheek where the icy hand of the night-creature had rested.

'Stay!' roared the swine-butcher as the others began to move. 'Stay — we have work to finish!'

Some cowered further away, others waited.

Thomas spoke briefly.

'The priest said it must be done in a certain way, then the thing cannot trouble us again — who will help, who amongst you is man enough to destroy the creature?'

'Will you be butcher?' asked the small man.

Thomas shuddered.

'I cannot do it,' he said simply. 'I cannot go near the fangs and the talons.'

Those that had made for the porch turned back. They saw the corpse-like figure of the woman had not moved again; but they saw too that the nostrils distended in time with the slight rise and fall of the exquisite breasts.

'What are we to do, masters?' asked the small man.

'Bury her deep!' Thomas said. 'And the small beast with her!'

'And the curse is gone?' asked some-one.

'I know not,' Thomas said simply. 'But the Holy Wafer blessed by the Bishop is here — let us seal the lead three times and place the Holy Wafer on the seals.'

'And mix the mortar with Holy Water!' called a mason.

'And use the Nail of the True Cross to hold the brass engraving down!'

'And then hide all under the alabaster,' said Thomas. He shook himself. He looked down at the dead priest once more. 'That done, we say nothing of tonight. Is it sworn?'

And now a shaft of pale weak moonlight did steal across the altar and towards the ice figure on the hurdle. As if in anticipation, the blue-veined eyelids of the night-woman twitched slightly.

There were men who recognized the danger. A brave man flung the grave-wrappings over the corpse, and this was the signal for a bout of furious activity in the chancel. Thomas himself took a chisel to the bright brass, gouging with all his strength. Within an hour, the only sign of the night's weird happening was the figure of the dead priest stark across his own altar and the gleaming white alabaster monument that hid the burial-place.

2

Sally burst into our crafts shop with the yell that means she thinks our fortune is made. I've heard it many times but we still had trouble finding the rent.

'Andy, we're rich! Leave that trendy junk and see what your beautiful true love has discovered!'

She wins no prizes for modesty, doesn't Sally Fenton, but she's truthful. I can't think where she gets her features and figure: her mother turns the scale at a hundred and eighty, and her father is a bald, skinny clerk with a face like the late Jimmy Durante (and if you don't know him from the old movies he's a nose and a set of ears looking for a weather-worn gargoyle). Sal is ripe and luscious of body, tall and big-busted, and with a heart-shaped face; she's blonde in the dull-gleaming ashy way of many German women; her eyes are dark blue, and she had promised to marry me when I got her

14

pregnant. She tells me she loves me, and I have to believe her. We had been together for four months.

I had met her at art school. We were both nineteen. After a few months of it, we counted our money, borrowed what we could and told our lecturers that we thought school was the last place for an artist to practise; fornication, politics and drugs, yes, but not art. Three agreed with us; one asked if he could come along when he learned our plans, and two said we were stark raving mad to give up the chance of freeloading for a few years. No one thought we should stay. We had to disappoint the volunteer — I'm not in the least liberal-minded when it comes to Sally — and we left to the cautious good wishes of everyone.

We had already found the place where we were to try to earn a crust. It was a stone barn built around 1710 and derelict. I saw that it would easily adapt for a crafts work-shop and saleroom, and that we could knock up a partition or two to make a bedroom and kitchen area. The farmer who owned it drove a hard bargain.

15

It was February when we moved in, and by March the place was habitable. That was when the first Peak District tourists took to their cars and sallied forth to buy expensive junk in the small towns of the High Peak. In the Middle Ages, robber-barons used to levy a toll on travellers who used the passes over the Backbone of England: now, it's the gift-shops. I didn't feel any compunction about joining them. If people want to buy plaster casts of gnomes at twice Woolworth's prices, why shouldn't they buy mine? We sold candles, too, garish objects in purple and yellow.

They went well at first. I also picked up bits of interesting junk from the industrial towns nearby — I had a regular arrangement with a couple of scrap-merchants. Anything that would go on my shelves they set aside for me. Chamber pots were highly prized.

We both did some painting. I went in for landscapes, Sal for rather moody pictures of horses. She was much better than me, and she had more ideas about stocking the shop.

When the craze for chalk-on-velvet came, she could sketch in purple volcanoes and green-eyed Eurasian girls with the best of them; we made some money that way, but when he saw how well we were doing, the farmer upped the rent.

We had little time for our own painting; I found I was wrong in thinking we could do more of our own thing in Derbyshire than at the school. We were busy from morning till night painting gnomes, producing instant antiques from the junk we sorted, and knocking off cheap watercolours of things like 'Mist over Mam Tor'. Don't get me wrong — I'm not complaining about the amount of work we did; in a way, it was very satisfying. We didn't charge the tourists too much, and if we saw that a customer really felt something about one of our bits of paintings and hadn't much money, we'd knock it down to half the asking price.

What we were looking for was a way to get a few thousand together quickly so that we could negotiate a proper lease on the barn, or find somewhere else where we wouldn't be subject to our landlord's gloomy rack-renting; so far we'd backed losers. I had invested good money in the velvet boom, but I had caught it at its tail end. Now, I had hundreds of assorted lengths of velvet that no one wanted: that was one of Sal's ideas. After that, came the potting-wheel.

Sal bought it in a sale. She'd forgotten that we didn't pot. It stood in a corner of the saleroom — it looked good, I must say, but it wasn't going to bring us any money; and no one wanted to buy it. Likewise our several hundreds of decorative candles. I don't understand the tourist. One week she — rarer he — will buy anything. The next they become choosy. Candles were in during the winter — everyone wanted candles, red and green, purple and yellow, pink and blue — we had them all; I had sweated for hours over the greasy pots. Now, candles were out.

So, when Sally burst in to say that we were rich, I treated it with some suspicion. Not that I showed it, of course.

I hadn't got her pregnant yet, and I wanted to make sure of her before I put on the dominant male image.

'Make us rich,' I told her. 'We'll buy the farm and throw Judson out.' He was our landlord.

'Mock, scorn me, revile me — I've made some mistakes, Andy, but this is the real thing. Catch!'

The thing brought bad luck at once. She had rolled it up in a tube of cardboard. In the badly lit salesroom I didn't see the damned thing until too late. It caught me squarely across the eyes, then it went on to knock over a shelf of plaster gnomes.

Sal laughed like a drain for five minutes. She had an excellent laugh — medium-pitch, sustained, none of your yelping gulps but a full-throated belly laugh. I began to see the joke when I had got over the sharp pain. We lost a customer just then, someone who popped a head around the door and retreated when he saw Sal doubled over the remains of a dozen gnomes; he mumbled something and ran for his car.

19

'For Christ's sake!' I got out when I recovered. 'What is it, Sal?'

'Your face — the gnomes — that funny man in the raincoat — '

'They're all hilarious, early Charlie Chaplin, great jokes but what's this you've found?'

'Open it! Oh, your *face*!'

It isn't a bad face. A bit on the thin side, but pleasant enough. Sometimes I think I have an Italian face — something Florentine. Maybe not. At least it was an innocent face in that Derbyshire spring.

I pulled the paper out of the tube.

'Brass rubbing?' I asked. I had seen only a corner.

'Of course! It's fantastic! We'll make a bomb, Andy! It's lucky I had some paper and a crayon in the van! Can't you see it — we can do a couple every morning before we open the shop — if we only sell one a week, we can live like in the Hilton!'

Her enthusiasm was infectious. I unrolled the rubbing and began to look at it closely.

As I've said, the place is badly lit. We

have two neon tubes high in the roof of the barn. The windows are high and don't amount to much, and anyway it was a miserable day. The hills were covered in mist, and the roof leaked in the two usual places. I shifted the large rectangle of stiff paper so that the rain wouldn't drip on it; there was more light on what served as a counter.

I saw the disfigured face of the woman first. I thought Sal had been a bit slapdash, but I didn't say so. There were two main figures, a man and a woman. Overall, the rubbing measured about five feet in width by about four feet. The figures occupied most of the space; there was the usual band of inscriptions set into the fancy border, but it wasn't this that I looked at. It was the woman. Her face, or rather the lack of it. It was missing.

Someone had scored out the lines of the engraving where there should have been features. What was left was a mass of gouged marking; yet even though the face had been almost obliterated, there were signs of beauty in the long-dead woman's neck and shoulders. The artist had had an eye for proportion; he had caught the graceful contours of her body with extraordinary skill.

'That's Sybil,' said Sally. 'He's Humph. Humphrey to the customers. Humphrey, Lord of Stymead. Sybil and Humph, come to make us rich.'

Did I sense the power of the dead? It's possible, though I think it might have been a certain exasperation as well as foreboding that made me say:

'It's no good to us, love. Sybil's incomplete. We couldn't get away with a faceless wonder, not even with the Yanks. Stupid they may be, but they know about faces. Now, Humphrey's handsome enough — we could do a line in Humphs.'

He wasn't handsome at all. The artist had tried, but Humph's portly, short body just wouldn't do. Where Sybil was tall and willowy, Humph was plain fat. In his hooped armour, he had the shape of a certain kind of ice lolly Sally was addicted to. I think they call it a Space-Whopper.

'It's going to be Syb and Humph,' said Sally firmly. 'We can't separate them.

Besides, it wouldn't take me much longer to do two figures once I've got the paper set up.'

'Sal, we can't sell them. Brasses have to be perfect. I know there's a good market, but no one wants a badly disfigured brass-rubbing.'

For answer, Sally winked. She took out a soft-lead pencil and made a few rapid lines on a sketchpad. There was no doubt that Sally had talent — far more than I. In a moment, a woman's face had emerged, a calm and peaceful face of the kind that is common on brasses. The woman looked back at me with a wonderful serenity. I pictured her face on the graceful neck and shoulders.

'Well?' asked Sally.

'It's cheating, but it's terrific.'

She and I grinned at one another. Any doubts I felt slipped away. We both knew we were cheating, but that's what the art world's about. Why shouldn't we put a face in the roughly-scored space where the Lady Sybil's face had been before someone got to work on it with a chisel?

Sally took a knife and scored along the

edges of the face. She placed the cutout over the brass rubbing. I nodded.

'It'll do, Sal. Now, where does it come from?'

Sally and I knew about brass-rubbings. They're a lucrative source of income for impecunious art students. Find a good brass, spend a few pounds on paper and rubbing-wax, and you could net yourself ten times your outlay, say five from a dealer. If the brass was rare the figure could go considerably higher. The trouble was that too many rubbers were chasing the few high-quality brasses left in the churches. Rightly, the parsons up and down the country were beginning to kick against the way brasses were being exploited.

'You won't believe this Andy, but it's from a derelict church a few miles from here. *And I'm sure it's an unrecorded brass!*'

That really was amazing. The Church has always attracted scholars, and the British Isles are particularly rich in ecclesiastics who have compiled lists of this or that feature of buildings: vestments, documents, ornaments, funerary and memorial inscriptions — anything and everything that can be listed and described. Non-clerics have added their contributions, so the literature of church architecture, furnishings and fittings is massive.

'They couldn't have missed a brass. Not an important one.' I didn't want to argue with Sally, but I had to. The likelihood of anyone finding a piece of engraving like this, one that wasn't listed somewhere, was extremely low.

Sal threw the van keys onto the counter.

'Just where do you think I've been all day?'

'I did wonder, my love.'

'I've checked three of the leading authorities on brasses. Not one of them lists it. There's no mention of a Humphrey or a Sybil of Stymead. Not one. I looked in four other books as well, but they're not systematically indexed, so it took me time. Nothing! We've got this to ourselves!

It was worth money, even more now.

I have slightly more than the normal

share of natural cupidity. Besides, I wanted to lay the best studio money could buy at Sal's feet. The rubbing was the only short cut to come our way.

'You're beautiful, intelligent and lucky,' I told her. 'Apart from having my heart in your hands, you have the wit to know when you're on to a good thing. You brought your find to me. By the way, where did you find it?'

'Stymead.'

'South of here?'

'East. Towards Chapel-en-le-Frith. There's a back road that leads to Hathersage eventually. I got lost and came across the village.'

'Far?'

'Ten, twelve miles. It's steep. The Ford got stuck twice.'

All the roads in the Peak Districts get to be steep after a mile or two. They wind as well. Our van was ancient, but it got us about. One of my friends at art school had given it me as an unwedding present: that's what he called it, so I didn't argue. There was a craze for Lewis Carroll at the time.

'But you got there.'

'Weird, Andy, weird! You know it rained this morning?'

I looked at the yellow plastic bucket in the centre of the salesroom. It was nearly full again.

'I know.'

'Well, I'd got a load of best quality antique junk from Barlow at Huddersfield — by the way, he wants another fiver, I didn't have enough with me, but it's lovely genuine stuff — where was I?'

'On the way back.'

' — and it poured! The road was awash! I had to stop, or I'd have floated down a mountainside. So I pulled in and just waited until the rain stopped.'

'It didn't.'

'I know. But it slacked off, and just as I was going to start the engine. I saw the ruin.'

'At Stymead?'

'There isn't much of Stymead. It's a pub and a post office and about a score of houses. But this was outside the village — on a bit of a hill about a mile from the buildings. It's overgrown with oaks and birches.' It would be, I thought. Small, stunted oaks and slender birches. 'And nettles,' she said, looking down at her ankles. 'Even at this time of the year. Bloody nettles everywhere.'

'So you couldn't resist having a look when you saw the ruin.'

'You know me, Andy, sweetie. I can't pass a castle or an old barn without looking inside.' She was right. After all, she'd found the barn we lived and worked in on one of her expeditions. I couldn't complain. 'Anyway, I went over the sheep wire and right into this very wet thicket. No one saw me go across the field. Come to think of it, I didn't see anyone at all in Stymead. It looks like a village under-water — you know, as if it had been left behind in a valley that was flooded. It was a bit like that going into the church.'

'What period?'

'Chancel from about mid twelve hundreds. I think part of the tower's a good bit older. It hasn't been used for a long time — no remains of Victorian pews. Just piles of rubble from the roof and smashed gravestones.'

28

'And the brass engraving.'

'And the brass. It was fantastic the way I found it. I got in through a gap in the wall — I didn't say the walls hadn't fallen in. They're still in fairly good condition to a height of say ten or twelve feet, but there's not much left of the roof. The porch is rather good. Quite a bit later than the chancel. It was a bit creepy, but not much. I daresay if it had been night time I'd have thought twice about going any further but it seemed all right at that time in the morning.' She paused, her brow wrinkling.

'Funny thing, you normally get birds in a thicket. Or a building. When it rains, I mean. They shelter.'

'And?'

'I didn't notice it at the time, but I didn't hear any bird calls.'

Our twin kittens woke up at that moment. They must have heard Sally's voice before, but they had been fed only an hour since, so they had decided to ignore her. We called them the Furry Queens. No separate names. I can't remember why. They made for her, wet as she was, and fawned about her ankles. She gave me an accusing look.

'They've been fed! And the dog!'

We had a large dog of mixed parentage that came and went as it pleased. We only needed a marriage licence to turn us into a properly domesticated household.

'Oh, you darling Queens!' Sally purred to the kittens. They purred back in the way female kittens do.

'You were in the church, Sal.'

'Creepy and a bit disturbing, love. Come to Momma, pretty little things,' she ordered. They did. 'You see, the brass was sticking out of a heap of roof struts — they'd fallen onto it.'

I could imagine the scene now. The rain, still wild in the heavy breeze, the slim figure of Sally Fenton bending over a blackened metal tablet, the mist swirling on the hills high above, and Sally exulting in what she had found.

'You had to clear the rubble?'

'It wasn't difficult — but, do you know, Andy, I think it had been concealed. There was quite a lot of rubble, but not all of it the kind of stone the roof had been tiled with.'

I should say that in Derbyshire the local stone was used to a couple of hundred years ago not just for the walls but for the roof-tiles of most important buildings. Slates came later.

'What sort of stone?'

'Alabaster.'

Alabaster is a strangely beautiful white stone, very hard and durable. It isn't easy to work, so it's expensive as a building material. Its main use is in funerary monuments. I wondered why an alabaster structure should cover a brass engraving.

'So what then?'

'I saw that I could clear the rubble away. It didn't take long. I knew it was good right away. The detail's terrific. Just look at the lion at Humph's feet.'

I hadn't looked at the animals. Usually there's a lion at the knight's feet and a lapdog at his lady's. Humphrey's lion had a half-snarl on its face, tongue protruding, and its claws threatened Humph's plump, armoured calves. Altogether a very proper beast. The lapdog was something else. Beneath Sybil's slender feet, a rather odd creature cowered.

When I say cowered I don't mean it looked afraid. It seemed to be hiding, as if it didn't like the light. A bit of drapery served to half conceal it, so there wasn't much of its face showing. One eye looked out of a squarish face. There was a disproportionately large muzzle. It didn't look like any dog I'd ever seen; I supposed that in medieval England they had some odd breeds. If Cornelius, our wandering hound, had seen it, he would have fled.

'The lion's fine, but the dog's odd.'

Sally looked at it thoughtfully.

'I thought so. It isn't in keeping with the rest.'

I thought of the prices we could ask and put down any thought of the beast's unpleasant appearance.

'Sally, I think you've got it this time. We can clean up on the Stymead brass. You say the church is derelict?'

'I don't think it's been used for a couple of hundred years.'

It was looking better and better.

Obviously no church ever crumbles away without being noticed — the church authorities are excellent guardians of their buildings; but, for some reason, this particular building had been allowed to fall down. It might be a lapse on the part of the diocesan authority, but it seemed likely that a decision had been made to let the place slowly fall apart. If no one was interested in it, then we would make a stack of rubbings and sell them on the stall later in the summer when we got the Americans, Germans, Japanese and Canadians — all would pay well for a bit of genuine English craftwork. As it was.

All we had to do was keep quiet about our discovery, and make our rubbings at times when we weren't likely to be seen approaching the ruined church.

The kittens decided to spring up at Sally — they think she's a sort of cat-goddess, and she might very well be just that, so what with one thing and another we shut the shop and listened to the wind and the rain in our leaky bedroom-lounge-dining room. As a sort of gesture to celebrate Sal's find, I put the brass-rubbing on the wall opposite the high window.

Sally wanted to paste onto it the sweet, serene face she had drawn for the disfigured image on Sybil, but somehow she didn't get around to it. In the grey light of the Pennines early evening, we lay close together, occasionally looking up with a smug satisfaction at the source of our good fortune.

Later we went out to the local pub. Sally attracted the attention of a party of rock-climbers. I found myself glaring at them, but they weren't impressed; she didn't seem to notice their flattering gaze. She had been rather quiet during our meal of sausage and beans — we aren't gourmets.

'Tired, Sal?' I asked.

She had been up early, and she looked rather pale.

'A bit, yes. But a thought's been bothering me ever since I got back.'

'What is it?' She was an impressionable girl, with the kind of imaginative powers that make me feel like a robot.

Her paintings — which are good

— have a deep sense of mystery. She does horses with wide, flat moorland background; the horses look lost, as if they were in a ghostland.

'Nothing — '

'The church? Is that it, Sal? It frightened you a bit?'

She shook her head. One of the rock-climbers looked hopeful. 'Not much. Not more than any old building does — there's always a touch of sadness about any ruin, but it wasn't that.'

She looked at me directly. Her deep blue eyes were almost violet-black. 'You know I come from Derbyshire, Andy? Not from here, but not too far away.'

Of course I did. I'm strictly a town bird, reared amongst high-rise flats and traffic. She was born in Sheffield, on the Derbyshire side. We had settled in the High Peak because she loved it there and I would go anywhere she wished. I liked it too.

'So what's the trouble, Sal?'

'Today — in the church — I had the oddest sensation. Only for a moment, and it didn't particularly frighten me. A sort

35

of chill but not the rain.' She leant forward and took my hands. 'Andy, I had the weirdest feeling that I've seen the church before.'

I knew what she meant. We all have these odd dreams when we're rambling through some strange place, and then months or years later we found ourselves in it and we say something like it's broken my dream. There's a fancy term for it and plenty of books about it. I told her what I knew.

She didn't smile, so I didn't make the rather silly jokes I was going to make. 'If you like, we'll go together to do the rubbings,' I told her.

'Oh, I'm not afraid of the church!'

Her vehemence startled me. The rock-climbers were interested again. They would be delighted if she quarrelled with me.

'That's good.'

We looked at one another rather uncomfortably. Only for a minute or two though. Sally has this way of knowing when a bit of physical contact is necessary. She wound her leg around mine and linked hands again with me. The rock-climbers recognised defeat and turned back to their beer.

We didn't talk about the rubbing again, not that night.

3

What amazes me in retrospect is the appalling speed with which the thing developed. The rubbing had been in our bedroom-living-room-dining-room for only a matter of hours before its frightful influence manifested itself. Not that I recognized it as such at first.

If anything, I thought that I was the victim of some oppressive dream — of the kind of sleeping sensation that had troubled Sally when she was awake and aware of what she was doing and seeing.

It started with the moonlight. I should say that the barn had a couple of chaise-longues, a vast leather armchair, a truly gigantic and imposing sideboard-cum-escritoire with magnificent carven ornamenting mainly of flowers and birds, oriental carpets, corner-cupboards in a material which the late Victorians tried to pass off as ebony, and, as a centrepiece a bed which was completely out of character with the stuff we had acquired from our junkyard friends. It was a gift from an eccentric aunt of Sally's. She had sent to France for it and paid hundreds. It was nearly circular, with a headboard in pink satin and plastic cupids. I hadn't met the aunt, but I already liked her. It's not the bed, or the aunt, or our junkyard furniture that I'm concerned with just now, though, it's a general impression to show how the room was arranged.

The bed was in the centre, as a centrepiece should be. The furniture was ranged around the walls. One wall, previously blank, had been decorated with the rubbing of Humphrey, Lord of Stymead, and his wife. On the wall opposite to them was the high, quite wide window of the old barn. We had cleared away the cobwebs and stuffed the cracks in the woodwork with plastic glue: the windows no longer rattled in their frames. There were no curtains, since neither of us had thought them necessary. The shutters were wide open.

When the moon was up high over the bald hills of Derbyshire's peaks, it struck into our living quarters. Now, it reached through and onto the brass-rubbing. Just the lower right-hand corner of the paper.

I noticed it because I had awakened from one of those dreams that you have to get out of because the results, if you don't, are calamitous; I didn't remember what it was about, but there was a terrible sense of loss remaining when I forced myself into consciousness. And when I did awaken, I saw the insidious, sly movement at the edge of the paper and identified it with the unhappy memories of my dream.

A strong white bar of moonlight lanced across the room. It hit the great-jawed beast full in the face. What was peculiarly disturbing was the way the creature seemed to be sliding into place amongst the crayoned folds of the dress which was its habitual place; I could have sworn that I saw the black-limned material descend around the thing.

I shook my head and turned to Sally. But she was asleep. I wanted to waken her so that someone else could confirm the horrible impression the creature had made on me. I didn't quite believe what I was seeing — if I had, in fact, seen it at all. By the time I looked away from Sally's tranquil face, I was already doubting my momentary image of the creature's slithering movement. I looked at it again.

The moonlight was much weaker. A high cloud partly obscured the white rays. The right-hand corner of the tough paper was only dimly illuminated. All I saw was a greyish blur, with a faint outline of the woman's long dress. I couldn't see the beast at all.

I wasn't afraid. I felt uncomfortable, but I thought that my disturbed state was due to the dream. I was puzzled, however, so much so that I slid out of the covers and walked across the cold floor to the wall. I didn't put the light on. Sally would have been awake in a moment. She hates an overhead light in her eyes.

I had only the poor moonlight to see by. As I got closer to the brass-rubbing, I was conscious of the cold. I was naked, and it had been a chilly day. The floor was bare wood. We had no heating on, so I didn't expect to be other than cold; but I felt so cold that my teeth started chattering, and I could feel the gooseflesh crawling all over my body. At the same time I was annoyed with myself, for I found that I didn't want to approach the enigmatic brass-rubbing.

'What's happening to me?' I asked. 'Damned if the cold's going to stop me!'

I took another step. The cold was more intense. It seemed that a miasmic breath encased me. There was a disgusting odour, which, with the cold, made me want to rush back to the warm sleeping form in the bed. Then the moonlight returned, stronger and harder than before. It hit the lower part of the brass-rubbing so that the black waxen images were harsh and clear. I saw the creature that had seemed to move.

Sally had made an excellent job of copying the original at this point. Hair, small eyes, wide jaw, pointed ears — all were there in full detail. But there was something else.

I reached out a hand.

'Sally — ' I said aloud.

I stopped and snatched my hand back.

'Christ!' I heard myself muttering. 'It *can't* be! It's not where it should — '

'Andy!' Sally called aloud. 'Andy!'

'Here, Sal!'

I was so relieved to hear the sound of a human voice that I turned away and leapt to the bed. The horrible attraction of the creature was over. My brain was free of the nightmarish ideas that were tumbling end over end in a frightful confusion. I burrowed into the bed and took Sally's naked heat with gratitude.

I didn't want to look at hangovers from dreams, and I certainly didn't want to endure that bitter cold of the early morning.

Sally was only half-awake — I think that she must have sensed that I had left the bed, and she wanted to know why. She shuddered as I pressed my cold body to hers, but she didn't speak. In a minute or so she was asleep again.

I lay awake for an hour or more. I kept my head well down under the duvet. I didn't look once in the direction of the brass-rubbing. What had happened was just a leftover of the dream

— I was sure of it. The creature had not moved. I told myself a thousand times that the lapdog was just that — a waxen image of a medieval pet that had died some five or six hundred years before, and that the slight movement I fancied I had seen was a trick of light and shade, caused by the effect of a cloud scudding past a part of the moon, or a cobweb drifting down from the rafters and casting a delicate shadow onto the paper as it fell to the ground. I tried to laugh at myself. Andy Thomas, big as the side of a house, hairy as Moses, twenty years of age and afraid of a bit of wax.

I didn't laugh, but I got to sleep because I was young and healthily tired. I didn't fall into that forgotten yet some-how deadly dream that had oppressed me. When I awoke, Sally was nudging me.

'Go and make the tea, Andy. I did it yesterday.'

'All right.'

Sally seemed surprised at my ready agreement. Usually we argue for half-an-hour about the tea-making.

'Didn't you sleep well?' she asked when I brought it.

'Not too badly.'

'You woke up, I remember.'

'Yes.'

I inspected the brass-rubbing. Not overtly, of course, since I didn't want Sally to worry about my imaginings of the night. There wasn't a thing out of place. The wretched little dog was where he should be, behind the folds of the dress worn by Sybil. He peeped out in a way that was simply mischievous, not furtive or threatening. Apart from his extraordinarily large jaws, he looked like some Rover or Rex or Rusty. He'd sit up and beg for biscuits.

He and his master and mistress were going to make us rich.

Sally wasn't to be put off.

'You had a bad dream. What was it about?'

'That you'd left me.'

As I said it, I knew that was what I had been dreaming. I could sense the cold tendrils of that dream reaching out to me in the bright morning. Sally pushed her tea aside and pulled me down to her.

'It was only a dream.'

But it had been terribly real, in the way that cruel dreams can be. I had a distinct memory now of one of the short sequences that had me awake and sweating and panting for breath. There was a mound of soil, a ring of angry faces; and a gaping grave. In the grave a rigid, silent form.

'Sally, it scared me!'

'It's gone. It's over.'

I sweated at the memory. So that was why I had been so ready to believe that the waxen impression of the dog and its mistress had seemed to be moving: I had undergone a severe strain whilst asleep, and so I was open to phantasmagorical imaginings.

I felt more relieved than I cared to say. I told Sally about it in a rush, making it seem screamingly funny.

'So there I was, barefoot and goosepimpled, looking at this terrier at three o'clock in the morning and thinking it was going to savage me!'

She didn't laugh.

'It wasn't just the dream then.'

'Oh Sal, I was only half-awake — you know how it happens. You're between sleeping and waking, and you think shadows are giants or witches or bug-eyed monsters from Venus. That's how it was.'

'It frightened you, didn't it, Andy.'

'Only for a few moments. If it had really scared me I shouldn't have got out of bed.'

'You thought you saw it move. How long was it moving?'

I wanted to drop the subject, but Sal was interested. She won't let a thing drop when she has that level-eyed look about her. And when she talks in the voice she was using now — calm and clear and a bit lower than normal — she sounds like a schoolmistress I used to revere when I was nine. Very sure of herself, quite certain she would be obeyed.

I told her the little I remembered.

'I only got a glimpse. But it looked as if it was thinking of going for a walk. Like Cornelius when he starts to scratch at the door.'

It wasn't the same. It was subtly alarming.

'Let's see,' Sally said. She flung a nightgown around her sleek shoulders and went across the room. I didn't want her to touch the brass-rubbing. But she did. She ran her fingers over the beast. 'You thought it moved. Has it?'

I looked more closely.

'It hasn't! I'm getting sick of the damned thing! Let's get rid of it!'

I reached out a hand to tear it down, but Sally grabbed my arm. Her strength surprised me. She has slim arms, thin wrists, and not much in the way of muscle; but she held my right arm back for long enough to make me listen.

'Andy, leave it! We might as well keep it. If we're not sure about making more rubbings, we can scrap the idea. Let's talk about it tomorrow.'

Reluctantly I agreed. Sally smiled at me.

'If there is anything queer about it, we can always check with the brass at the old church. Wouldn't you like to see it?'

'No. I don't want anything to do with it.' I didn't like her continued interest in the thing. However, she could always persuade me that some new venture would be successful, no matter how unlikely the prospect. And I began to remember the value of brass-rubbings.

Gradually, my latent fears and suspicions were overcome.

'I'll tell you what we'll do, Andy,' Sally said. 'We'll go out to the ruined church later on — in the evening, after shop hours. How's that?'

I grumbled and Sally cooked me a huge breakfast. Eggs, bacon, sausages, tomatoes, beans, the whole works. Afterwards, I went out to price the vanload of junk Sally had brought in yesterday.

Cornelius returned halfway through the morning. He was wet and hungry. I gave him two cans of dog meat, which he wolfed in a minute. His big head remained cocked on one side in the diffident begging way that means he's not even half-full. Normal dogs eat one can a day. I gave him two more. After that he went to sleep. I had every sympathy with him. He was courting a rather stupid collie bitch.

The day passed unexcitingly, though towards late afternoon we got a rush of customers. Several of them bought pictures, which pleased Sally. I bargained over a pair of Victorian vases with a small Asian. He won, without much trouble. By the end of the day, we had made more than enough to cover costs.

We had a good meal at a modest restaurant near Sheffield, with two bottles of red wine. We don't drink as much usually; so as the Ford swayed back over the winding roads we sang pub songs and talked about painting. Our unusually profitable day caused us to forget about the brass-rubbing and the ruined church. We didn't think about Stymead and its long-dead knight and lady. We were concerned with ourselves.

Both of us slept well. I awoke about seven to see sunlight blazing through the high window. It was going to be one of those spectacular spring days when the Pennines look like the posters — a patchwork of last year's bracken and green meadow, with silver and blue streams and grey rocks; cotton-wool clouds hung above the flat-topped hills in the bluest of skies. There were even larks about. Everything cried of spring and youth.

Sally hadn't opened her eyes. Probably she was wondering if she could get me to make the tea for the second day running: I got out of bed and she sighed contentedly with the soft satisfaction all women show when a man obeys their unspoken demands. I opened the door to the shop to let the kittens in.

'No sugar, darling,' said Sally. 'Or maybe one lump. Say two, and I'll give up cream in my coffee. Two lumps and an aspirin. That wine!'

I heard and didn't hear. I couldn't credit what I was looking at. Sally's voice was only a part of the general background noise, like the birdsong and the distant baaing of the lambs.

Sally was waiting for the hiss of water in the kettle and the rattle of our immense breakfast cups. She didn't expect my loud roar of disgust and horror.

'Ugh!'

'Andy!'

She sat up, following my gaze. I walked through the doorway as one of the kittens hurtled past me, its tiny voice a screech of protest.

I looked at the other kitten. It was dead.

I didn't wait to explore the avenue of thought that began, most horribly, to take shape in my mind. The kitten struggled in Sally's arms. Sally knew I had discovered something horrible. She ran; I was too shocked to have the wit to hide it from her.

Her shriek echoed and re-echoed around the high, old barn. It rang against the high rafters and was hurled upwards by stone walls and cold floors.

Then she was holding something in the hem of her frothy wrap. A bloodied scrap of fur, with staring blue-green eyes, a thing weighing hardly a pound or two, for it was drained of blood.

And she held it to her face.

She sobbed and whimpered, and so did the remaining kitten. The birdsong from the fields provided a reminder of the rest of the busy world outdoors, but I was altogether bound up with our private grief. Some feral creature had entered our home and ripped out the kitten's throat; and we had slept throughout.

I felt a furious frustrated anger against the silent thing that had invaded our privacy. I thought at once in terms of the hunting animals of the night — of a fox that somehow had crept into the shop through an open window; of a wide-winged owl, beak bright red with the kitten's life-blood; or a weasel squeezing through a gap in the ill-fitting boards.

For a moment or two I wondered if Cornelius had snapped angrily at the kitten (they tormented him, had done so since they came to us); but no. Cornelius had not returned from his wanderings.

I tried to comfort Sally as best I could, and it was with thoughts of making her a cup of tea that I turned back to go into the living room. It was then that I saw the marks on the brass-rubbing.

When I saw the blur on the black and white rubbing I knew at once that something ugly had invaded our lives. I have excellent eyesight. The colour showed up red-rust in the sunlight. There was a streaky daub of redness where there should only have been black wax or white paper. I reached out to touch the lower right-hand corner of the picture. The dog's jaws were obscured. Its long fangs were hidden by the dried compound. When I touched the stuff that had left a sticky matted covering I knew at once what it was.

I wasn't able to speak coherently.

' — but how could it — ' I was saying, I badly needed a rational explanation.

I shuddered and wiped my hand on the edge of the stiff paper. A long red streak made a lurid exclamation mark beside the image of the blank-faced woman. I felt like retching.

Then I exploded with the word I had tried to keep back:

'Blood!'

Behind me I heard Sally speaking. I turned. She placed the dead kitten on a small table.

'Andy! What is it?'

I pointed. 'On the dog — on the

rubbing — *there*!'

'Here?' She was beside the hideous blotch, and reached out her hand.

'Don't touch it, Sally!'

She did. 'It's paint.'

'No! It's blood!'

She turned to me. 'Blood — how can it — '

'I don't know! But it's there!'

A thin mewling sound attracted Sally. She bent. 'Poor puss!'

I looked at the waxen dog and at the living creature in Sally's arms. The kitten nuzzled for comfort into her neck.

'Sally,' I said in a quieter voice. 'It's real, and it is blood. Paint doesn't clot like that.'

'But how did it get there?'

I went back to look at the brass-rubbing. Without flinching, I reached out to rip the ghastly thing from the wall, but again I felt Sally's hand on my arm. Her strength was amazing. I had never guessed at the steely power in her slender arm. She actually held me back.

'Leave it,' she whispered. 'Andy, I couldn't bear it if you touched it!'

We both looked up at the empty space where the face of the woman should have been. It seemed to call us, as if some distant long-gone echo of a past rang out. I felt Sally trembling beside me. And then the blood of the kitten began to congeal on my arm.

I held back my anger. And my fears. But nevertheless a furious resentment smouldered within me. I was angry with the feral thing that had killed the kitten; with myself for my unstated and unacknowledged fears; with the brass-rubbing for mocking me so obscenely, daubed with blood.

The only thing I couldn't be angry with was Sally. Her grief brought her to a temporary collapse.

So I was angry with Cornelius and kicked him when he came back from his nocturnal love-making at the Harris farm.

When I had buried the kitten's remains, Sally began to recover.

'How could the blood have got onto the rubbing?' she said. 'Do you really think there's something wrong with it?'

We were out in the small patch of land

that I was trying to turn into a vegetable garden. The sun was up, it was after nine o'clock, and we expected customers soon. I thought about my answer. I didn't want to alarm Sally unnecessarily, but I didn't want to utter the kind of soothing platitude that would have satisfied most women.

'It might be my imagination. I had that bad dream. Not last night, the night before.'

'When you thought you saw the dog move and I wouldn't believe you.' She was apologising.

'It's not your fault, love. You can't be responsible for my nightmares.'

'And you think the dog moved in the moonlight?'

I thought about it. 'Yes.'

'I haven't looked at it properly since — since last night. Shall I?'

'You're all right now?'

I had wiped most of the blood off.

'Yes.'

'Then let's look.' We went into the room. The sunlight was brighter than before. It all looked so innocuous, our ridiculous French bed with its cupids, the breakfast cups and discarded paintings.

The black and white rubbing looked harmless. Only one streak alongside Lady Sybil remained, and that could have been mould.

'Well?' I asked Sally. 'Was it the shadows?'

'I made the rubbing, so I should know. But I can't tell.'

I looked at the dog's fangs. I wondered if my imagination was playing tricks on me. 'Sally — '

'What, Andy?'

'I could swear its fangs weren't so prominent, not yesterday or when you brought it.'

Sally decided things for us.

'We'll go now.'

'No. We can't just close the shop.'

But we did.

4

Sally seemed more excited than anything else as our old van groaned up the hills and clattered down into the switchback valleys. She had recovered from the shock of the kitten's death. There were none of our customary jokes, but she didn't seem either depressed or alarmed.

The day fulfilled its early promise.

There can be few places on earth more beautiful than Derbyshire in the spring. I sometimes complain about the trippers who clutter up the hills at the weekends, but I can understand what draws them to the shallow hills of the Pennines. It can be bleak and raw even in July, but when the sun shines on the pastures and the great stretches of bracken and heather, especially on an April day like that one, then it is utterly beautiful. The air is fresh, there are small bright bowers if you look for them, the lambs have a wobbly agility that is comic and endearing, and the clearing mist over the higher peaks adds a quiet mystery to the scene.

There wasn't much traffic once we got off the main Manchester road. The odd lorry, a Post Office van, two girls on bikes, that was all. And there was no hint of life in Stymead. As Sally said, it looked like a deserted village. Only a thin tendril of smoke curling into the blue sky from one of the cottages gave any hint of human habitation. The pub was closed, of course. I looked across the road. There was a small shop with a letterbox set into the wall. The window had been painted green to about half its height. I saw boxes of cigarettes and sweets piled high in the dimness beyond, so I supposed that it was a general store catering for the villagers. But it looked dusty and neglected.

'It's a mournful place,' I said.

'Wait till you see the church.'

'I wonder why they stopped using it?'

'See,' said Sally. She pointed to an ugly redbrick building half-hidden by mountain-ash. 'That's a chapel. I'd forgotten about the Wesleyans. They'd be chapel people hereabouts. They'd have no use for a church after Wesley had been here.'

We motored on for a short distance, and I saw the mound. Through the twisted oaks and the birch I could see the ruin as Sally had described it. She was right. There was a melancholy absence of life about it that was almost eerie; no birds disturbed the budded branches. I remembered the gruesome blotch on the brass-rubbing and I shuddered again. I stopped the van at a grassed verge, but I didn't switch off the engine.

'Sally,' I said. 'Couldn't we forget the whole thing? Just drop it?'

But she was already opening the door.

'Come on, Andy! I want to know if you're right!'

She wasn't apprehensive in the least. I put her bright, excited air down to a desire to know more about the mystery of the place. I myself was persuaded to go on because I was still furious about the death of one of the Furry Queens. The remaining one would mope. So I followed Sally across the scrubby meadow, wet from the night's rain, to the nettle-banks and the heaps of fallen stones. I tried a joke:

'We could try to rent the place if Judson throws us out, Sal. It has to be cheaper than the barn.'

Sally turned to me, her face for once disapproving.

'Live here! What a horrible idea!'

Then she was ploughing through brambles and undergrowth towards a long, weather-rotted wall. The thorns whipped back at my neck and arms. I cursed, and the silent thicket absorbed the sound of my voice like a great green blanket, Strangely, for it was a warm morning, I felt a chill entering my body; Sally called for me to follow and then she appeared to vanish.

'Sal!' I yelled irritably. 'Sal!'

'Here!' she answered, and her voice was faint, as if it came from miles away.

I went on and stumbled over a knotted root. When I recovered my balance, I saw a gap in the wall. It had been concealed by a couple of bushy hawthorns. I squeezed past adding a few more scratches. Crumbs of rotted mortar stuck to my sweater. There was a slimy deposit, the product of many years of decaying vegetation on the fallen masonry in the gap. I couldn't help feeling that Sally must have been unusually interested in the place, for she disliked getting her feet wet.

She was standing at quite a distance from me when I saw her. There was enough of the walls of the tower to cast a deep shadow over her. She was wearing a dark trouser-suit, leather boots, and a dark scarf around her hair. In the gloom of the ruin, I had a momentary impression of a funereal figure. Sally could have been a mourner at the long-dead couple's grave.

She heard me and turned:

'Isn't it too much, Andy? Don't you get the feeling that almost anything could happen here?' She was excited. I should know, since I have seen her in all her mercurial moods. Sally was living through sensations that simply don't happen for most people. She was alive to her fingertips. Her voice was vibrant, her eyes sparkled, and her lips were brilliantly red.

If we had been anywhere but in a religious building, I should have grabbed her to me.

'You know, it's as though I were part of it, Andy! I can't help feeling I know this place as well as I know the barn — in some ways better! I could almost describe the church as it must have been when it was standing!'

I didn't want her to try. If I had had a hint of what was to come, I should have pulled her from the church and taken her as far as we could go; as it was, I had a strong feeling that she should not be encouraged in the belief that she was in some way associated with the ruined church, even if it was only through a half-remembered sense of dreaming about it. To distract her, I said what I thought was something practical and sensible:

'This would be the chancel.'

'Yes!'

'And this is the tomb?'

I walked towards where she stood. I had to negotiate a few heaps of rubble to reach the cleared area in the deep shadow. Sally pointed to a dark metallic rectangle.

'Humph and Syb!'

'The dog?'

'Look.'

I looked, Sally must have spent a considerable amount of time in clearing out the dust and dirt of centuries, for each line of engraving was sharp. The dog's hair, small mane, ears, eyes and fangs were almost as the engraver had left them. It was not remarkable that the rubbing had been so clear. I considered the engraving with a professional attention for a few moments. I didn't want to think about the question that had drawn me to the place, not yet.

Sally said sharply: 'Well, Andy? Has it moved?'

'What do you think?'

'You know what I think.'

I studied the folds of the dress with care. We should have brought the brass-rubbing, I found myself thinking. That way, we could have compared the copy with the original.

But we had left in such a hurry that so

obvious a precaution simply hadn't occurred to me. Or to Sally.

'It looks like the rubbing,' I said at last.

It did. I had an image of the rubbing in my mind's eye, and I trusted my memory. You have to be able to fix a scene in your mind if you want to paint, and I had that ability.

'Then it's all right, Andy,' said Sally, and she was looking at me with sympathy and understanding.

'It looks like the rubbing does now,' I said.

Sally's face showed only sweet reasonableness.

'I don't follow, Andy.'

I was going to tell her that the wretched dog looked exactly as it should — that both the rubbing and the original coincided; but that I thought, incredible as it would sound that both seemed to be slightly different from what I remembered of the rubbing when she had first showed it to me. I didn't tell her. I was so exasperated by a combination of things that I wouldn't say anything at all of what I felt.

'Forget it!' I said, and the loud tones echoed back from the half-fallen walls of the tower.

'If you say so, Andy.'

'And I don't want to take any brass-rubbings.'

'Then don't.'

'And I don't want you to come here again.'

'I won't.'

'And I'm going to burn the bloody rubbing when we get back. I'm sick of ancient churches and lost brasses!'

She was being altogether too reasonable.

'As you say, Andy.'

'And stop agreeing with me!'

She smiled at that, and I felt the familiar heart-catching excitement. Her teeth gleamed white, her lips were a vivid red, and her cheeks sparkled with health. She was so freshly and invigoratingly alive that I felt the spell of the dismal old ruin evaporating under her own particular form of physical magic. All my gloomy imaginings were dispersed.

I didn't analyse my thoughts at the time,

but I suppose I must have dismissed the appearance of the blood on the brass-rubbing as something easily explained. After all, we lived on the edge of one of the great wet deserts of England, where hunting beasts still stalked their food day and night. The kitten was a casualty of an unceasing struggle for survival; so how could one harbour resentment for long, when birds and beasts must hunt their prey to live?

Nothing out of the ordinary had occurred. Nothing.

'I suppose I might as well have a close look at the brass.'

'Only if you want to, Andy.'

I examined the brass. 'It is very good, isn't it?'

'Brilliant.'

'Can you read the inscription?'

'Only the easy words.' Sally came closer, and we both knelt in front of the tilted slab of brass. 'It says *Dom.* there. That's *Master* or *Lord* of the place. That refers to Humph. He's called *Armiger*. It means *Knight*.'

'What does it say about Sybil?'

'I can't make out the words. I gave up Latin in my second year at school.'

'I suppose it's unimportant.'

'I suppose so,' agreed Sally. Then she said: 'I could find out.'

'How?' I was to curse myself for asking.

'There's the library. And I've got a girlfriend who did Classics. She'd be able to translate from the rubbing.'

'Which I'm going to burn.'

'After I've shown it to her.'

'All right.'

'And they hid the brass under an alabaster monument,' said Sally. 'I wonder why?'

I was tracing the outline of the lion at Humphrey's feet at the time. It was excellent, like the rest of the engraving. I thought of the lapdog at Sybil's feet and I stretched out my hand to trace the lines it was composed of. I couldn't touch it. Not even fleetingly. I got up, and Sally repeated her question:

'I wonder why they hid the brass, Andy?'

'Hid it?' I was trying to rid myself of my distaste for the lapdog.

'They concealed the brass. Someone did.'

'Someone defaced Sybil,' I said. 'I can't make any sense of it.'

'She was hated,' Sally said quietly. 'You wouldn't do that to the representation of a person if you didn't hate them.'

'No,' I agreed. 'But it was all a long time ago. I suppose we'll never know.'

I had made up my mind that I didn't want to become rich through brass-rubbings; not of Sybil and Humphrey anyway.

I turned and I caught a sudden movement. I saw a small whitish face and an intent stare. Someone had been watching us through a lower window of the ruined tower.

'Good God!' I said.

Sally turned instantly. 'What, Andy?'

I was six strides away by then, I leapt over piles of masonry, bits of the tower-roof, and over what might have been an ancient stone cross, now shattered so that only the massive central section was left; then through a tangle of small bushes, until I reached the narrow window where I had seen the face. I looked out onto thick undergrowth. It was still waving; some was broken down. I heard a crashing from the edge of the thicket.

Sally was beside me then.

'What is it? Someone watching?'

'Yes! I don't know who.'

'He went towards Stymead.'

'Yes.' The trail of swaying and crushed undergrowth led to the sombre village. 'Maybe one of the kids,' I said.

'Kids wouldn't come out here.'

I shrugged. 'Come on, Sal. It's been an experience. Let's leave it at that.'

She looked back to the brass tablet. 'It's a pity to leave it there. It's going to be covered with leaves in the autumn, then the nettles will come, and it'll be forgotten.'

'Yes,' I said firmly. I made myself believe it. 'Let's have something to eat — but not at the Stymead pub.'

We went through the sombre village on our way to a hamlet a few miles from our barn. I thought I saw someone watching us as we passed the pub, but I couldn't be sure. It was an unremarkable building, stone like most of the cottages, but it had an odd sign that I couldn't see clearly.

'Black Nigget?' she said. 'What's that?'

'Never heard of it. Why?'

'The pub's called The Black Nigget.'

'Odd name for a pub.'

'Nigget,' she repeated. 'I've heard the word before.'

We didn't talk much, and when we had lunched we decided to go back to the barn to open up the shop.

It wasn't really worth it, because the tourists aren't in the buying mood. An enthusiastic Australian almost bought one of Sally's paintings, but he decided against. 'Never get the bleeder back in one piece,' he said cheerfully as he left 'I like it though. She's got talent, has your girl.'

Polite admiration wouldn't pay Farmer Judson, so we talked about ways of raising cash. Not that we were especially hard up at the moment — we'd had one good day that week; but I think we both felt that we couldn't rely on Judson if once we fell behind with the rent. So we decided we wouldn't needlessly antagonise Judson. If necessary, I could raise a loan from my parents, but I was in the first flush of independence and I disliked the idea.

One thing I wouldn't hear of was brass-rubbings.

'There's always Humph and Sybil,' said Sally.

'No!' I shouted

Sally sulked until about nine o'clock, when I suggested we got out to the pub. She threw pots into the sink, smashing a perfectly good dinner plate and a cracked mug

'You shouldn't shout at me!' she said angrily.

'I'm sorry about the bloody brass-rubbing, Sal, and I'm sorry I got edgy this afternoon. But I'm not going to keep on saying it!'

'You're shouting again, and you said you'd burn Humphrey and Sybil. I spent hours doing the rubbing.'

'So OK, I won't burn it!'

'You'll tear it up.'

'I'll leave it where it is!'

I looked around helplessly, until I found myself staring into Humphrey's face. His eyes were closed, of course. I began to wonder if he had endured such scenes: or were men made of sterner stuff in the Middle ages? He didn't look especially chauvinistic, though the engraver had given him a resolute chin. I couldn't make up my mind about him. Certainly he would have needed to keep an eye on Sybil; she was much too lissome to leave behind for long when he decided to go crusading. I looked at her scored-out face and wondered what she had seen in Humphrey. I smiled at this, recollecting my earlier hostility towards the brass-rubbing. How stupid it seemed now!

Sally was ready for a truce. She produced a bottle of Italian wine she had been saving. We had canned spaghetti laced with shreds of green pepper, and later we strolled to the pub. Sally was in a tender mood, and I was immodest enough to enjoy the frank envy on the faces of the men in the bar. She gave me such languorous glances that I was almost embarrassed. It was the last time I was to be totally and unreservedly happy.

We went home hand in hand.

5

Sally insisted that the surviving kitten sleep with us. I didn't object, but then Cornelius tried to snuggle down into the duvet. He came back three times, and finally I grabbed his flabby hundred and thirty pounds and heaved him out into the night.

He made straight for the Harris farm, though he did look back with one reproachful glance.

'Goodnight, Lothario,' I called after him. He wagged his tail and we parted friends.

'I wonder what 'Nigget' is,' Sally said when I got in beside her. 'It has to be something, Andy. I've heard of Black Bulls, Blue Boars, Red Cows and Green Dragons. But not a Black Nigget.'

'Forget it.'

I turned off the light. I lay awake, listening to a couple of loose tiles that rattled in the wind. It was a cold night, with the chill coming from the top of the peaks where there was still the odd patch of greying snow. I dropped off to sleep thinking about the ruined church and the silent village, but I didn't sleep for long. Something awakened me, a hint of movement or a slight noise, or perhaps the tiles shifting position high above.

Sally sighed in her sleep as I lifted my head.

I saw the moonlight slicing across the room to the foot of our glorious bed. It showed up one of the plastic cupids with a strange blending of white and gold. I thought of the mixture of metals the Greeks favoured, the one made up of gold and silver called electrum. Then I looked beyond and watched the moonlight on the brass-rubbing.

I had never known the condition which we call 'terror' before. It's something far beyond fear, for it's unreasoning. I suppose you can say a child is terrified if he wakes in the night, as I did, and finds some unnatural sight or sound which he is unable to account for; but, for most children, there's the safety and comfort of the bedclothes and the warmth of the cuddly toy beside them, and apart from these immediate assurances, there's the knowledge that two loving adults are nearby, well within call, both competent to deal with the bogey that's only the shadow of a curtain or the mysterious creeping noise that turns out to be a rosebush's untrimmed branch brushing the window. Some children get quite a thrill from this kind of thing. Maybe I did, but I can't remember any details. Certainly, I had never known anything like what I felt. Not blind, mind-bending terror.

My mind exploded in one stark, wild rush. I was paralysed by terror. I couldn't move, not even to scream. All I could see was the dog.

The moonlight was a steady beam, as rock-steady as a searchlight. It hit the brass-rubbing with a flood of silver-white radiance. And, in the moonlight, I saw the dog. It was writhing. I could see it as plain as I could see the white-gold of the ridiculous cupid at the foot of the bed. The dog was writhing, a long-haired thing with legs like four snakes and a body that glistened blackly in the stark white moonlight. And the thing was moving about the folds of a black and white gown of some rich and heavy material like brocade. I didn't see just the one ear and the half-concealed face: I saw the whole of the animal or apparition or night beast. Heavy head, long and sinuous body, and the short slithery legs. And the fangs. I saw it all, the entire thing.

A part of my mind that had nothing to do with reasoning accepted the fact that there had been a transition from immobility to movement: that the frightful snaking movement was taking place. It was my artist's instinct, this, to try to compare the eerie happening before me with some phenomenon of a similar kind in my own field. If there was one, it was some kind of trick they use in the discos-strobes, maybe, to enhance the effect of a girl dancing. In the discos, they can give her four or six dimensions, when they're good. It was something like that now. A flat, two-dimensional, very ordinary brass-rubbing had taken on a flowing, solid shape. There was depth in the grotesque happening before me, depth as well as height and width. It was a solid, corporeal creature.

Sally's rubbing of the Lord and Lady of Stymead was alive. The lapdog was crawling towards the blank-faced woman's bosom. And as it crawled, a low and unholy slavering sound came from it.

I could not move, not a single muscle, but I had to have air, I was choking with the effort to hold back my breathing so that the slight movements should not attract the attention of the beast; I took in a sobbing breath that seemed to me, to roar around the high barn with the force of a whirlwind. The terrible thing showed no sign of having heard. I could have wept with relief. And some of the frozen terror slipped away.

The violent and surging emotions I felt did something to break the hold of that overpowering and ghastly sensation, and I could ask myself questions like how and why. And I could tell myself that the manifestation I had seen the previous night was not the natural phenomenon I had preferred to believe it. I had seen the slight movement of the beast. Its position was different from what it had been. I had witnessed the first stirrings of something that defied any rationalising, and I was now seeing a development of it.

As to what it was — what the beast from the engraving could be — I could not and would not begin to guess. The memory of that ultimate state of mind I had just undergone was too fresh for me to dare to ask for an explanation of the writhing, whimpering, slavering, creeping huge-jawed monster's presence. It was enough that it had shown no interest in me. But I could give some kind of half-explanation of why it was making its way upwards.

The moonlight glared now, a white radiance that was cold and eerily beautiful. I could see haze-motes, so powerful were its beams. And I could see the stuff of the woman's dress: not waxen crayon, flat and immobile, but a heavily-textured woven cloth that hung in subtle folds to show the elegant lines of the body beneath. There was a slight stirring of the dress, and I saw that the hazy dust motes were flickering as if they were affected by a breath of wind; the frightful beast let out a low-pitched growl, and I detected an almost deliriously happy quality in its tones. I might have asked myself now how this could be, but I began to lose the slender grasp I had on my own faculties.

I knew why the lapdog was moving so steadily upwards, for, just as it reached the woman's covered bosom, I saw the sleeve of the dress move and then a slim hand. White and blue-veined, the hand had as much substance as my own. There was a hand, a slim wrist, and the material covering the arm. I felt my breath freeze inside my lungs as the hand slowly reached down to the over-large head of the night-beast with a gentle, authoritative deliberation. Then the hand pushed the fearful creature's head against the breast.

From the sounds the thing made, I knew that it had accomplished what it had set out to do. I closed my eyes against the incredible and ghastly sight, for my unreasoning terror was back with me. I had seen the dead arise, and I felt despair in my soul.

How long I stayed like that, immobile and bitterly cold, I can't say. I do know that there was a rustling noise from the wall where the awful brass-rubbing hung, but it soon stopped. I might have stayed in that half-hypnotised state for ten minutes or an hour, even two hours. Simply, I could not move. I wasn't conscious of Sally's presence, nor of her existence. If she stirred in her sleep I didn't notice it.

The howling brought me out of my trance.

I don't know how long I remained without moving, but I recall hearing the distant sound of three solemn notes on the bronze bell of the parish church; and, almost immediately afterwards, the long, wailing howling that broke my spell of extreme terror.

It was a horrific noise. I knew that it did not come from the throat of any animal of the English countryside. Such sounds had not been heard in the High Peak since the last wolf was hunted to its death. There was violence and fury and a wild eagerness in the howl that had nothing to do with the stoats and weasels and night-hawks of the Pennines. Paradoxically, the sound did not increase my terror. It may be that I was at some strange stage where I could only pitch into madness or retreat into normality; as it was, I reacted by shuddering and groaning with pain and a return of the anger which had possessed me when the kitten had been slaughtered.

I was frightened and bitterly angry. This time, however, my anger was directed not against myself but against whatever noisome graveyard creature had invaded my home. I opened my eyes.

The whole room was changed.

Where there had been sharp and clear shadows, there was a grey mist of unclear, swirling shapes; the moonlight had lost its power. It was soft and pearly, but grey too, and there was a dampness that was almost visible, as though droplets of water hung in the moonlight. I looked for the brass-rubbing and its grotesque figures. It was half-concealed in the eerie vapour.

I eased my cramped limbs. I felt the bed take on a slightly different shape as Sally moved in her sleep; she made a small contented noise. I looked for her face but the beautiful ashy hair concealed it in the strange light, she looked like a woman seen at the bottom of a river through reeds. I shivered at the thought and forced myself from the bed.

No incorporeal manifestation was going to drive me to such heights of terror again. I was sure of it. Anger pushed me forward one step, two steps. All about my cold body I felt the cold seeping through my skin with an insidious force. Cold, clammy mist hung to my chest and arms. I seemed to swim forward rather than walk. Images battered against my mind. The moonlight on the night-beast. The hand, slender and comforting, on its frightful head. The needle-like fangs, and the slavering sound from the great jaws. And, horribly, a blank space where there should be a serene face.

How I managed to take another two steps is beyond me. I put it down to my phlegmatic nature. Sally is the one for fancies and the wild excesses of imagination. I am a plodder, stolid and persistent, the kind of person who sets his mind to a task and will not be deflected. The mist closed about me and I reached out my hands blindly. I sensed opposition.

I could feel the power of the thing now, very strongly. There was a menace in the miasmic, clouding, choking pearl-grey stuff: I could feel the presence of a will opposed to mine, and whatever uncanny sepulchral thing it was, it knew my intention and was determined to stop me. The unwholesome miasma entered my throat, a vile, clinging vapour that made me retch with nausea. I had visions of winding-cloths and rotting grave-cerements, of corruption and rotting detritus, and, at the same time, of the eager slavering jaws of the night-beast. But I would not be defeated, not now that I had conquered the terror that had afflicted me. I pushed forward towards the wall.

The mist began to shred away, and the moonlight faded to a thin grey smoke. I found myself coughing like a bronchitic as I expelled the foul vapour. Two or three more steps now. The cold struck through my bare feet. I brushed against the chair Sally used for her clothes; it squeaked and settled after rocking dangerously. I could see the oblong of the rubbing, but no details. The figures were part of the greyness.

And then I was a yard from it, my hands outstretched to tear it down. I would drive out the phantoms and their grotesque writhings, utterly destroy the thing that slavered, root out the vile grave-creatures. My hands shook, though, and my arms were locked. I could see the corded muscles of my arms, and the hooked fingers so near the heavy paper. I strained, but nothing happened. And then I was fighting for breath again as the frightful miasma caught at my throat!

Something had enwrapped my nerves, stifled my breathing, destroyed my resolution. I heard a low fierce sound and knew it came from my own throat; and then an answering tiny noise, as if a silvery note had been struck. The small sound stuck in the thick air, and it chilled me through with fear once more. I said something. I don't know what, but it was cut off by a great scream.

It was my own scream.

I felt a hand on my cold neck, I felt small, sharp talons, and I screamed out in anguish as though I knew that the night-beast had come behind me and leapt for my unguarded back.

Then warm hands pulled me, and a warm, naked body thrust itself against mine, and Sally was there, Sally calling to me by names we used only when we were making love but this was right for I needed the reassurance of all that was precious to me.

'Sally!'

I said it again and again, and she answered me and I knew that the mist had gone once she touched me and, with it, the whole terrible manifestation. I clung to her, sobbing and shaking like a child, she saying little as I recovered. There was no mist and none of that grim moonlight. I never thought to have welcomed darkness before, but I did then. It was the harsh moonlight that was the dangerous time. I knew it with a great, indelible certainty

'Come to bed,' Sally urged. 'Come back, Andy! You're frozen.'

'Yes,' I stammered at last. Then I thought of the monstrous images I had seen. 'No! Put the light on, Sally!'

'What's happened? What is it, Andy?'

'Put the light on!'

'All right, love.'

'Keep hold of my hand.'

'Come with me, then.'

I didn't dare let go of her. I had recovered in part, but by no means sufficiently to dispense with the tactile reassurance of another human being. I did not care to be alone. I dared not let her go.

'Why were you out of bed, Andy? Were you sleepwalking, do you think? I heard you scream — it was terrible, Andy!'

'Put the light on.'

Sally hugged me and then she switched on the light.

I looked down at her and saw shocked concern in her exquisite eyes. She smoothed her hair from her face and stared at me for a few seconds. I had a crazy thought then.

'The kitten! Is she all right?'

'She's on my side of the bed.'

I looked, but I felt my eyes sliding along the floor so that I should not have to look towards the wall where the brass-rubbing hung. The kitten let out an almost soundless mew of puzzled inquisitiveness, and I watched it stretch itself, its small pink mouth and tiny white teeth making a huge yawn, a ridiculously wide yawn for so small an animal.

'Andy?' Sally asked.

'Yes, it was a nightmare.' How could I tell her what I had seen? How could I inflict such a gruesome story on her? Already I was trying to bring my reasoning faculties to bear.

'About the church and the brass-rubbing?'

'Something like that. You startled me.'

I couldn't tell her of my terror. A man doesn't confess that he was beyond the far reaches of reason. She patted me, I thought rather absently.

'So that's why you were out of bed.

How do you feel now?'

'Cold.'

'Shall I heat some soup?'

I heard the parish clock strike five. Soon it would be dawn. 'Yes, love.'

'Was it bad?'

'Yes!' And I found that I could share my terrors, for the conditioning that tells us that boys don't cry and are never afraid was broken. I couldn't keep it to myself. 'I saw Sybil's bloody dog!'

'That one?'

I could not look. 'Yes. How does it look to you?'

'One of the bits of sellotape has come off. Shall I put it back?'

My mind lurched. Another easy explanation for an apparent psychic manifestation? Was it another case of the untrimmed rose branch tapping against the window, or the cobweb drifting down and making strange shadows in the moonlight? But I could not look. I could not turn my head to examine the rubbing. I had seen the night-beast, solid and eager, and I had seen the white hand caressing it as though it had accomplished some clever trick.

'Tear it down!'

I had been paralysed. My hands, which are large and muscular, had not obeyed me, neither had my arms been able to reach out for such a simple task.

I heard paper rustling and sellotape tearing from the plastered wall. And still I could not look.

'I'll put it in the tube,' said Sally.

'In the shop.'

Sally heard the odd tone in my voice, but she acquiesced without comment.

When she came back, I asked again: 'How did it look?'

She turned as she opened the can of soup. The kitten got interested in the prospect of food.

'To tell you the truth, Andy, I didn't look at it. Not properly. One corner was folded over. I rolled it up and put it in the tube straight away. Shall I get it out?'

'No!'

I breathed a sigh of relief and felt normal and hungry. The first hints of daylight were in the room, and there were the noises of a working village around us — a noisy cock bawling to his rivals; a dog barking impatiently at a late fox. It was all over. I had a stack of dead branches and garden refuse to burn.

'Soup's ready, Andy.'

'Good! I'm going to have a bonfire later, love.'

I felt delighted now. I was going to burn the brass-rubbing when the sun was up.

6

The smell of bacon cooking awakened me. Sally, I thought. The room was rather gloomy. I sensed rain in the chill air as I levered myself up on one elbow to watch Sally at the stove. She was humming to herself, a pleasant little tune which I couldn't put a name to. My gaze wandered across to the wall opposite the bed, and I felt a jerk of apprehension as I saw that the brass-rubbing was gone.

Then I remembered that Sally had removed it. 'Where did you put the brass-rubbing?'

'On the shelf above the last of the gnomes.'

'I think I must be going crazy.'

Sally turned and smiled indulgently at me. 'You look a bit woolly at the edges, but you'll do.'

'I did see the dog move.'

'Eat your breakfast.'

My appetite was unimpaired, but I saw

that my hands were shaking slightly as I forked the bacon and eggs into my mouth. I didn't want to think about the flowing movements of the night. I hadn't the trick, however, of putting things out of my mind. Sally can shake off the glooms. I can't.

We didn't say much over breakfast, but when she was cleaning the pots away, Sally told me she was going out for the morning. It wasn't unusual, and I was half-glad to have her out of the way. I assumed she was going to look at junk or make some sketches for her next batch of paintings.

'Be back for lunch?' I asked.

'About then, Andy. You're sure you're all right now?'

'Oh yes.'

Once the brass-rubbing was burned, I was safe. We didn't discuss the events of the night. I thought Sally had decided it was better this way. She went out cursing the rain, looking like something from *Vogue* in her white boots and plastic raincoat, and when I heard the van chugging away up the lane I felt unutterably lonely. I didn't let my depressed state of mind affect my decision.

The cardboard tube was where she said it would be. I lifted it out and knocked down a moon-faced gnome at the same time. I didn't look inside at the brass-rubbing, feeling that I was handling something potentially dangerous, like a sleeping reptile. I put my boots on and went out into the mist and rain to the pile of garden rubbish I had gathered together over the past weeks,

I didn't expect to get a fire going at once. There was a little petrol in a can, so I sprinkled the wet branches and heaps of miscellaneous rubbish with it; I found a can of some oily mixture, perhaps someone's sump-oil. I was careful to give the tube a heavy coating of the black liquid. I stood back and threw a match at the heap.

The petrol exploded with a satisfying *whump!* and the thick oily liquid added a pall of heavy black smoke, with some small yellow flames. Weeds and branches dried rapidly, and the rubbish began to burn. I felt a blessed sense of relief. Squirming night-beasts, the thick accumulation of haze-motes, the delicate white hand — they would be half-remembered perhaps even comic recollections soon. I watched the oily smoke gathering over the cardboard tube. For five or ten minutes I kept a close watch on it.

I was disturbed in my vigil by our landlord.

'Where's that dog of yours?' he demanded.

He startled me, and I felt a tremor passing through me at the sound of his harsh voice. I turned and he pushed his ugly, aggressive head forward. His normally pink and white face was mottled, and his vast stretch of nose and lower jaw had the slightly zany look of one of his own sheep. He took my shivering for a sign of weakness.

'Dog?' I repeated, gathering my wits.

'Aye, that bloody dog of yours! It was out on the moors last night!'

'Cornelius?'

He grunted in annoyance. 'Whatever you call it! Where is it?'

I am slow to anger, but I can be roused. His peremptory demand was quite in keeping with his previous treatment of us, but he had not appeared quite so uncouth before; and he had caught me at a bad time.

'You'd better tell me why, Mr. Judson.'

'Because one of my lambs is lying with its throat torn out!' he bawled, and he was more sheep-like in appearance than ever, with his long head and face, topped by a coating of curly grey hair, thrust forward in righteous anger. 'Now where's your bloody dog!'

It was a serious matter. I could sympathise with him. Townspeople bring their pets out onto the moors and show them that the sheep and lambs are defenceless, trusting creatures; and, as a result, some dogs turn sheep-worriers. They have been known to form packs and travel for miles from their town homes to meet at night and become something far removed from their daytime selves. I remembered the ghastly howling in the night, and I shivered again.

'Cornelius isn't here, Mr. Judson,' I

said, 'Did you see him out last night?'

'Not me — Harris!'

'That would be right. He's after their bitch at the farm. But Cornelius isn't a sheep-worrier, Mr. Judson, You've got the wrong dog. I'm sure of it.'

I wasn't sure, of course. But I dismissed the idea that Cornelius had produced that wailing, ghastly sound in the night.

'We never had no lambs killed till you came with your fancy woman!' Judson grunted. 'But you'll pay — I'll have the police over, and you'll pay!'

'If it was Cornelius, I'll pay,' I said. 'But don't say anything about this to Sally, will you?'

I was very near anger now. He was a much older man, and I recognised that he probably had little experience of people who chose to live outside the conventional mould of his own kind; yet I wasn't going to listen to insults. He backed away. I knew then that he hated us, Sally, myself and now our dog.

'We'll see what the police have to say!' he snarled.

I didn't say anything. Instead, I turned back to the fire and watched the yellow flames turn to red and the black smoke give way to a lighter, hotter smoke. I thought that our problems — my problems — were over.

Surprisingly, I had a good morning in the shop. I even managed to sell a couple of views of the peaks that I had dashed off during our slack period a week or two back. Business was looking up. I felt comparatively cheerful by lunchtime, and I was expectantly glancing at the door every few minutes in the hope that Sally would burst in, her face alive with some new enthusiasm, when I had the feeling that I was being watched.

It wasn't the hair-on-my-neck-prickling thing at all, yet I knew at once that I was under observation by someone who had no interest in our wares. I was showing a Birmingham couple a maker's mark on a piece of Victorian pottery when I became aware of the intent stare of the man.

I caught his glance and he looked away. He was an odd looking person. I guessed him to be about thirty years of age, but he could have been older. He was of medium height, very thin though, with dank hair which glistened wetly. He had a bad case of acne. There was something vaguely familiar about him, however, and I wondered if I had a dissatisfied customer on my hands. They come back sometimes, not often fortunately, to complain about a fractured gnome or a chip out of a piece of pottery. One old lady once brought back one of our plaster gnomes with a complaint that it winked suggestively at her. We gave her a picture in exchange. I finished with the Birmingham couple, who didn't or couldn't make up their minds, so they said they'd be back later, then I asked the man if I could sell him something.

I was right in thinking he wasn't a casual shopper.

'Came to say it's village land,' he said.

You get this kind of taciturnity in Derbyshire. There's almost a spirit of competition in terseness, with sentences as short as possible and words clipped into monosyllables wherever it can be done. I didn't know what he meant, and I said so. The feeling that I had seen him before was very strong.

'Church is on village land,' he said, looking me straight in the eye and emphasising his enigmatic remark by pointing a finger at me.

'What church?'

'Old church out of Stymead!'

Of course. The ruined church and the watcher. I had seen his retreating back, glimpsed it more like, when he had scurried away in the direction of the village.

'Is it?' I said.

'There's no right of way!'

I was being warned off. I recognised the tone of voice. Much of the High Peak is National Park land; there is a network of public paths. But where there's no recognised right of way, the farmers fiercely defend their property. I didn't quite know how to handle this stranger. It wasn't like dealing with Judson — he was my landlord and I had to take care not to antagonise him unnecessarily; on the other hand, it seemed that Sally and I had trespassed.

'It's your land, is it?'

'It's the village's! It's ours. And we don't have anyone on it.'

I weighed the matter up. I had been challenged, in a sense. A total stranger had told me that I must obey him. He had taken the trouble to find out who we were, and now he was here to tell us that we had trespassed. I didn't want trouble.

'We won't be going out to the church again,' I said. 'It was just idle curiosity.'

'Missus too?'

'I'll tell her.'

He looked relieved and he relaxed his strained manner. I could see that he had been afraid, but I didn't think I was the cause of his tenseness.

'Best left alone,' he offered. 'Best left.'

'It was the brass that interested us.'

He shuffled, uneasy once more. He nodded his head in the local gesture of farewell and went to the door. As he opened it, Sally tumbled in, wet and radiant, just as I had hoped she would.

She lurched into the thin man, knocking him sideways and sending her shopping bag and its contents skittering over the floor. He didn't apologise. He looked at Sally without the usual open admiration of most men, and then he went out into the rain.

'Who was that!'

'He came to say we're not to go to the Stymead church. It's private land. I expect he owns the land.'

'He didn't look like a farmer.'

I thought of Judson then. 'Sal, Judson's been here. He thinks Cornelius has been worrying lambs. He didn't say he'd seen him actually chasing the lambs, but he says it's Cornelius.'

'He must be out of his mind!'

She threw off her coat and gathered together the tins of food she had brought. I helped, but I was feeling depressed again. It may have been tiredness — I had slept only fitfully — but I had the clammy sense of oppression once more, as if the rain had seeped into the shop.

'Anyway, where *is* Cornelius?'

I didn't know. He was frequently absent like this, and I had assumed I suppose, that he would be coming back famished and friendly at the end of his courting spell.

'I'll go see.'

I looked up the lane that led to the Harris farm There was no sign of Cornelius. I couldn't see much of the fields beyond, because of the mist. I turned to go back to the shop but on impulse I went to the smouldering embers of the fire. As the little drops of rain fell on the grey ashes, they made a sizzling noise. I tried to discern the shape of the cardboard tube. Vague suspicions troubled me. Why should the man with the pitted face take the trouble to come out personally to warn us off the church? Judson had told me that he would complain to the police about Cornelius: that was the correct procedure. If the villagers at Stymead objected to our presence at the ruin, they should have done the same. I felt that I had been altogether too humble towards the Stymead farmer, that is, if he was a farmer. I felt that I didn't want to be reminded of the Stymead church and the terrors of the night.

I had burned the brass-rubbing. It was all over. So why should I feel that I was still involved in the Stymead business? My wretched analytic mind wouldn't let it go. Phantoms: the ruins: a terse warning that the place was best left alone. Sally didn't help.

She spoke at length about Judson's evil-mindedness and then she became quite intrigued by the Stymead man's call.

'Didn't he say who he was?' she wanted to know.

'No. And I didn't think of asking him.'

'But what *right* has he to warn us off?'

'We had to cross a field to get to the church. It could be his land.'

'But there had to be a pathway from the village to the church at some stage — there must be a right of way.'

'What does it matter, love? We won't be going again. I've burned the brass-rubbing this morning.'

'You did!'

I could see that she felt a little piqued. I didn't blame her, for she had spent time at the brass, Nevertheless I wasn't going to have her sulking.

'You don't really mind, Sal, do you?'

'No!'

She looked thoughtful, however, when she brought in some sandwiches for lunch.

'I went to the library this morning Andy. I was a bit intrigued.'

I felt the return of the night's indigestion.

'By?'

'I found out what a 'Nigget' was. It's been running through my mind since we saw it at the Stymead pub.'

I didn't want to hear anything at all about Stymead but I couldn't squash Sally. 'What is it, Sal?'

'It's an old English word that isn't used any more It means 'a familiar'.'

'A witch's pet?'

Sally smiled. 'Yes. Isn't it weird how it all comes back to Sybil?'

7

Sally was in one of her quiet moods for the rest of the day. She found domestic chores to occupy her when she wasn't attending to the customers, so we didn't say much to one another. I recognised that she was still a little annoyed with me, and also that Cornelius' non-appearance was causing her some distress; for myself, I was quite glad that we needn't discuss the Stymead business. Had we been less busy, I should have told her of my past fears and also my present apprehension; and we might well have quarrelled, for I could tell that she was extremely interested in the history of the church and the couple buried there, whilst I wanted nothing more than to forget the place.

We went to bed early. I remember looking at the space where the rubbing had hung and feeling tremendously pleased by my own resolution. I said to Sally that we needn't have a Middle Age couple staring at us all night and she smiled back at me as though I had made a good joke. We were both very tired and with that we went to sleep. I can't remember dreaming, but I did hear the church clock brassily strike the half-hour when I woke. I couldn't guess what the time was. Half-past-something. Twelve, two, four? I didn't reach out for my watch — I was only half-awake. I recall thinking of Cornelius. He had been away from home for a night and a day, which was stretching it even for him. Then I opened my eyes and saw the moonlight.

At first it was just moonlight. The whiteness of it appealed to my eye, and I was trying to remember an Early Dutch painting I had seen in London the year before, one that almost captured the intensity of the moonlight which was flooding from the high window, when I found myself beginning to experience the blankness of mind that is the first symptom of the ultimate form of fear, stark mind-freezing terror. I recognised the cupid, white more than white-gold. I sensed that Sally was sleeping, for there was hardly a disturbance of the duvet to show that she breathed; I knew that the kitten was in a deep sleep too, for I could feel its tiny weight on my legs. The haze-motes were different, though.

They were not the slowly-rising, spiralling, sometimes descending dust-flecks which normally flecked the moonlight. There was something more substantial about the gathering minute particles that appeared in the centre of the glaring white light. They made a coruscating but somehow heavy column of white shadows. Gleaming with an unholy radiance, the particles coalesced, each finding a place in a tall, narrow and cylindrical space. I had seen such a shape before. There was a grotesque familiarity about it. It was like welcoming a friend back from a car smash, the impossible happening and a fellow-student who had been grossly rent in a motorway carnage suddenly appearing before one: I was in the grip of the night-terror again. The impossible was happening.

The dead were undead. And the undead was here.

Slowly, with deliberation that seemed all the more menacing for its slow care, the shape took on substance. Haze-motes became specks of white flesh. White flesh took on the casual elegance of the limbs. A long-gowned figure in rich dark material emerged, and so deliberately that I felt my mouth opening and then widening and then becoming parched as the terror spread throughout every part of my body; and still the ghastly shape of the undead thing acquired more and more of the appearance of a vital creature.

I was staring at the woman from the brass-rubbing.

The Lady Sybil de Latours had risen from her five-hundred years interment. I was looking at the physical shape of a woman who had been dead for five centuries of our era. I believed it. No phantom inhabited our living room. I believed at once and with all my heart that I was seeing the woman just as the artist who had engraved the brass had seen her, just as the women who had bathed her body had seen her, just as the craftsmen who had laid her body in the coffin had seen her; but she was alive, that was the difference.

Alive?

Some idea of what was happening tricked into my mind. As the folds of the heavy material she had worn to her grave began to sway gently with the movements of her slender and elegant body. I realised that I was in the presence of a form of manifestation that represented a frightful danger to me, to Sally, to all of the human race. It was no ordinary ghost, no gentle presence that appeared to me. I knew it at once, though I had no acquaintance with what is called spiritualism or black magic or sorcery — I know they are not the same thing, but they have this common element, that they dabble with things too dreadful for contemplation, too dangerous to face for long. This was no gentle sprite, no kindly thing looking for a local habitation amongst creatures it had known when on earth. It had come back from the grave. It was a *revenant*.

An echo of the Stymead man's words penetrated into my mind. *Best left alone!* With that echo, and with the return of a fragment of reason, came a reaction. It was not an intellectual thing. I didn't make any assessment of what was happening. I looked for a face, saw only an unsteady haze of white particles where there should be a face — and I made the sign of the cross.

It is an instinctive gesture amongst those brought up on the modern fringes of Christianity. I crossed my hand in front of me in a half-paralysed gesture, and the movement stopped. There was no further hint of the movement of soft flesh under the brocade. It was as though I had, in turn, paralysed the thing that stood before me. I shuddered. And Sally let out a small eerie sound.

I had not realised that she too was staring at the thing from the ruined church. I half-glanced towards her. There was a fixed and excited expression on her face. I recognised the look she had worn when she mentioned the meaning of the pub's name. There was a glint in her eyes that told me she was experiencing emotions quite different from mine. She didn't look afraid at all.

The horror of it struck me afresh. Sally was hypnotised by the gowned, blank-faced thing in the room. And her fascinated stare seemed to give it fresh impetus. Its life-like blue-veined hands came up in a small beckoning gesture.

'*Sally!*' I bawled her name with all the force of my lungs.

I felt her give a great shudder beside me.

The moonlight was a shining, deadly flood, brighter than ever. I watched Sally's face. She seemed to blink, almost to lose the intent and half-blind stare that she was directing at the terrible shape, and then she succumbed again to whatever spell it was able to project. I felt her slender body stirring. And her own slim arms came out of the warm bed and copied the beckoning gesture of the long-dead thing from the grave.

I was far too dismayed to repeat the sign of the cross. Sally, my girl, my woman, was responding to the invitation of the thing. I turned now towards her and watched the amazing concentrated expression on her face. She had never worn quite such a look before. I had known her in the most exalted and intimate moments, watched her too, but this was something again.

And I quailed at the intensity of her wild delight.

There was a rapport between the creature of the night and Sally that I found both disgusting and horrifying. Yet I felt that I had been aware, dimly, of this possibility; Sally's vivid imagination, her ethereal paintings of ghostly horses, her sudden impulses to be alone in ancient hill-forts or long-forgotten ruins, all were contributory indications to this obsessive excitement she was exhibiting. I waited appalled and helpless.

I could not bring myself to shout again. I knew there was worse to come, so I remained stiff and still as I had the night before, far too terrified to intervene even when it was Sally in the spell of this thing from a silent and haunted ruin.

Sally had the rather constrained movements of the sleepwalker. It was as though she felt the first symptoms of cramp; when she moved, there was little fluency, rather a kind of robotic precision about the play of her muscles She pushed the duvet aside. The thing in the moonlight waited.

Its arms came down, softly, easily, white and delicately marbled in the harsh moonlight. There was a strange shadow about the head. No face. No sound. It was as cold and silent as a winter's night in a graveyard. And Sally was in its power.

I couldn't see what she was doing for a moment or two. Sally had her back to me as she slid from the bed and took a step towards the white phantasmagorical thing. I watched the folds of the nightdress and wondered at her delicacy of figure. She bent over the bed, and I felt a slight weight removed from my feet.

I looked and saw what she had done.

In her hands, she bore the surviving kitten. The sister of the poor creature whose throat had been torn out two nights before by the night-beast. There was a grotesque inevitability about the sequence of events now.

Sally's eyes were riveted on the elegant moonlit figure. And the kitten still slept.

She held it before her for a moment or two. And then she advanced, and as she did so it let out a tiny mewing sound that was as pitiful a thing as I have ever heard; but Sally stepped forward again, lifting the tiny bundle of fur to her bosom, offering it comfort for a moment or two and then stretching out her arms so that the tiny thing looked up at the terrible white presence.

Vivid images smashed through my brain. I remembered the torn throat of the other kitten, and the bright red blood on the waxen image of the night-beast. I thought of its cruel fangs and its over-sized jaws.

I rebelled, even against my terror.

What I could not do for Sally, I could do for the helpless creature in her arms. I conquered my ecstasy of terror and moved my stiff limbs. Not towards the kitten — that was beyond my small powers of resolve. Not towards Sally, either, for to reach them I should have to approach the swimming, solid, evil thing. No. I have a slow mind, not much imagination, but I have a practical bent, I knew what I should do, and I knew what I could do.

It was the moonlight that was the danger. Moonlight brought the monster rearing up from its dusty wrappings. The white flood of brilliant light gave the undead thing substance: it's not just the horror movies that tell us a thing like that. No. It's an instinct, this distrust of the false light of the night. Moonlight is dangerous, deadly, evil. I had to prevent the light shining on Sally and the kitten: and especially on the ghastly, blank-faced manifestation.

I turned my back on the eerie scene and fumbled my way towards the wall. We had a set of ladders there, quite high enough for what I wanted. I felt my limbs jerking convulsively, partly through cramp, partly through the cold. My thoughts whirled, but my inner core of well-balanced, unimaginative attitudes and instincts held me steady, both in the literal sense as I swayed up the ladder and in the figurative sense, for I was a prey to all manner of additional fears now that I was committed to opposing the monster that haunted us. I envisioned the white hands and the blank-face as reaching towards me; a chill at the back of my neck half-convinced me that long fangs had brushed against me; I thought of the crawling night-beast that writhed so detestably in the deadly moonlight. But I did what I set out to do.

The old shutters had not been closed for years. Yet the rusted hinges gave as I pulled on the old oak, and I felt a grim happiness, for I had confronted the thing. I exaggerate, for I had hardly dared leave the seeming safety of the bed, and when I did leave it, I made sure that I did not look at it fully. But at least I had summoned up the courage or desperation to intervene in whatever ghastly rituals it was planning. I was in a tremulous, frenetic state that had more than a little of triumph about it. The shutters closed, and the moonlight was cut off as suddenly and completely as lightning dying on the horizon.

The kitten squealed, and that was all I heard, for I lost the careful balance on which I had been congratulating myself and plunged outwards into the black pit of the room. I had time, in my fall, to think of the shimmering deadly thing. Not much, but enough. My arms flailed twice. Then I hit the ground and knocked myself unconscious.

8

I must have been unconscious for a considerable time for I was thoroughly chilled in every bone when my own groanings awakened me. I didn't remember what had happened at first, so I must have been mildly concussed. I felt a burning pain in my right leg as I moved. My outstretched hand touched the wooden ladder. Chinks of light in the doorway and at the high window showed me where I was: quite near our bed. I looked about me and saw the bright eyes of the kitten staring at me hopefully.

I cried out in relief.

As I did so, the horrific scene blazed in my memory. Deadly white moonlight, evil glamorous thing fresh from an ancient tomb, Sally bearing the scrap of pulsating animal towards it; my head rang with pain. My mouth was flooded by bile. I almost vomited where I lay.

The kitten scrambled down the side of

the duvet and came to me. Its trust overwhelmed me. I could have wept when it ran a pink tongue over my hand. And I knew there was no danger, not now. Not in the daytime. The undead walk at night.

I thought of Sally then.

Sally!

I got to my feet, testing the damaged right leg. It held so it wasn't broken, not even badly strained. I jabbed on the bedside light and wondered what I should see.

Sally was asleep.

I have said that she is beautiful. She is. There can be no question about her beauty, wide-set eyes, a nose of delicate proportions, a firm chin, high cheekbones, all this surmounted by hair of an ashen sheen that can be subtly exquisite in its own right. I had never seen the tiny smile, though not the one I saw then.

The corners of her lips were curled, very slightly but enough to give her a mocking, insincere, knowing look. And yet she held her beauty. She was Sally still, so beautiful that I felt my heart miss a beat when I saw the rise of her bosom under the duvet; but the beauty was flawed.

She had seen the evil of the night. It had not terrified her. She was different from what she had been. There was a loss of innocence in that tiny smile. She awoke as I trembled at the thought of her danger. I wondered what to say to her.

'Andy, love! Made the tea?'

I was expecting surprise, fear, terror even: a reaction to what she had seen. Her commonplace request floored me.

'What time is it, Andy? It's so dark in here!'

I pointed upwards. Surely she knew?

'Who shut those bloody things!'

'Me, of course.'

'They spoil the room! I said so when we moved in! They block the light!'

'Yes.'

She knew. Surely?

'Well, don't stand there, my own. You look frozen.'

'I've been out of bed for a while.'

'Then make the tea or get back in. Preferably both.'

'All right.'

I couldn't touch her. She was playing

some terrible game with me. Surely?

'Cuddle up, Andy, you're Arctic! Talk about frozen flesh!'

I let her wind her soft body about me.

'Aren't you well, love? Couldn't you sleep? Andy, you've not been having those nightmares again!'

'Sort of.' I hesitated. Was it possible that I had imagined it all? No! But had I? And if not, surely she recalled something? I thought of her stiff movements. Sleep-walking? 'Did you dream?' I asked.

'What of?'

I ran my words together in my frustrated anger:

'Of a woman like Sybil! Of a woman made out of moonlight! Of a woman who wanted you, Sally, or the kitten, or anything warm and full of blood, Sally! For God's sake, darling, don't you remember walking out to her — I saw you, Sally!!

She disentangled herself,

'Saw me? I'm sorry, Andy. I don't follow.'

'Sally, in the night I woke up and watched you get out of bed, pick up the kitten and take it to the woman.'

The words sounded absurd. They made no sense, not in the morning. I remembered how foolish I had felt after that first manifestation — half-believing in it, the rest of me almost contemptuous of myself. Sally didn't think it was absurd. She was quite serious.

'You really saw this, Andy?'

'I did.'

'And I walked towards a ghost?'

'It wasn't a ghost. It was real. It was as real and solid as myself.'

'Sybil?' She said the word like an incantation.

'Yes! It's her. Sally, for God's sake, we're haunted by this thing!'

She half-smiled. I saw a faint likeness in the smile to the sly, knowing upturn of her full lips that I had seen when she was asleep. That was when I began to be afraid, not for Sally, but of her. It was only a beginning, however. My immediate concern — my overwhelming concern — was to protect her. First, I had to point out her danger.

She didn't seem impressed. 'So Syb

doesn't sleep too well,' she said lightly. 'I expect she was a lively lass in her day.'

'Sally, it's not a joking matter. If you can't remember what happened, you were sleepwalking. That, or she hypnotised you.'

'She hypnotised me! Andy, really!'

'You took the kitten to her.'

Sally stopped smiling. 'You're not suggesting that what happened the other night was — '

'No! I don't know what happened the other night! All I know is that there was blood on the rubbing around the jaws of the dog-thing, and that I burned it yesterday. I don't say you had anything to do with it, and I'm not saying you took the Furry Queen to her in the night — not intentionally, anyway. But I do think you're under some kind of evil influence, and I think we ought to treat it as a diabolically serious matter.'

She put an arm around me.

'You've been working too hard. It's this place, out in the hills. It does that to people who're not used to the Peak District. It's easy to imagine things. I do.'

'It isn't imagination.'

'Nightmares? Or even the old barn. It's full of echoes of the past. The human mind's a strange thing, Andy. You might be receptive to the vibrations here when you're asleep.'

I couldn't believe any deception to be in her. She spoke softly and sincerely, a good friend as well as a lover. I had misjudged her. The smile was a nothing.

Yet I had seen the woman from the grave. No amount of dissuasion would convince me I had not seen the white hands beckoning. I spoke my piece.

'Sally, it started when the moonlight touched the — the dog. It isn't a dog! I'm sure of it. There's the look of a wolf about it.'

'It isn't pretty. And anyway, why didn't Syb have her lapdog with her last night? Was it just her you saw?'

'She was enough by herself.' I hadn't thought of the night-beast. I shook my head and had to lie back as the pain raced through it.

'Head bad?'

'I fell down the ladder.'

'Poor thing! Oh, Andy, what a night you've had!'

I accepted the comfort of her arms again.

'I fell off the ladder, Sal. I was closing the shutters. It was the moonlight. First on the dog. That started it all. Then, the night before last, it shone on the woman too.'

'And you shut out the moonlight?'

'It gives them life.'

'Them?'

'Sal, the kitten was *drained*!'

She wasn't horrified. My earlier doubts about her returned. Normally, women over-react to the thought of wounds, death, mayhem, and especially blood. She looked down at the kitten on the duvet and poked it with her finger.

It looked at her, mewed and then, quite deliberately, spat in her face. Then it ran for the shop.

She laughed, but I was afraid. Nevertheless, I kept talking.

'Judson's lamb had its throat torn out, Sal. I don't think Cornelius did it.'

'He's not been back for two nights now.'

I didn't think of it right away, but she hadn't defended the love-struck dog.

'Sal, I think the moonlight gave them life.'

'Them?' she said again.

'The woman. Her beast.'

'Moonlight on a picture — on a brass-rubbing!'

I backed away from the idea then. The way Sally said it, it sounded as though I had come out with some vile suggestion: it was vile, but it was suddenly unreal. She has great power over me, has Sally. She has the ability to make my thoughts run into new channels so that I can share her sometimes strange and soaring ideas. And she can apply scorn to my gloomy imaginings.

'It sounds far-fetched, I know, Sal — '

'It sounds idiotic. I'll make the tea.'

'You haven't been there again, Sal? To Stymead — the ruin.'

'No. Why should I?'

'But you went to find out something about it.'

'I did, yes. There's a bit in a nineteenth-century history of the Peak.

Stymead Church was a monastery for a while then they rebuilt the church and it served the parish. Then no one used it after about the middle of the eighteenth century. It just fell down.'

'Wasn't there anything about Sybil?'

'No. Should there be?'

Was she being altogether too innocent?

'I'd have expected a mention of the family.'

'There wasn't, love.'

The kitten mewed from the doorway, but it wouldn't come near us. Sally didn't seem to notice.

'I'd have thought Sybil — and her nigget — would have been mentioned.'

'Drink your tea. You're getting obsessive about it all, Andy. Why don't you go out for a long walk? Go over Mam Tor. It'll clear the cobwebs out of your head. You don't look a bit well.'

'I'm all right.'

I was trembling slightly. I was more and more convinced that Sally had become enamoured of the ghastly thing that haunted us; and I knew what I should do.

I pretended I was going for a walk,

though I took the precaution of saying I'd look in on one or two people to see if they'd seen anything of our wandering dog.

'Andy, don't worry so much,' said Sally. 'I'll be all right, love!'

I was going to make sure. I had known by instinct how to ward off the spectre or corporeal thing of the night — by the power of the cross. But how to make sure that it no longer plagued us was a matter for the expert. I went to see the local Anglican priest.

I hadn't met him before. We weren't churchgoers, though Sally had quite a strict upbringing in the Anglican faith.

She had lapsed since going to Art College, and I had parents who were unthinkers rather than freethinkers. I was reasonably confident, however, that the priest would help us. He was a grave and dignified man, seen from a distance, which was the only way I had seen him so far. He ran a Mercedes and I had heard that he was quite a monied man in his own right.

I knocked at the vicarage door. The

vicarage, which I had time to study whilst I waited, was set back in a pleasant piece of parkland, well away from the rather busy Sheffield road; the church looked to be about thirteenth century maybe early fourteenth. Its square tower was uncompromisingly Derbyshire; there was little in the way of ornamentation: no carved buttresses and only a relief in flowers above the porch. The vicarage was a more ambitious affair or perhaps only more ostentatious. It was mid-Victorian neo-Gothic with little turreted towers, cast-iron fancywork on the roof, a great timbered porch that was riddled with woodworm, and mullioned windows. On a board I saw the vicar's name: I. C. J. Cunningham, M. A. I knocked again my inspection too protracted for my liking. And again.

It took ten minutes to rouse the vicar of St. James's. When he came, I knew I had chanced on one of the English eccentrics. We breed them, and they gravitate towards the professions. Law, politics, the Army. And the Church. I've known one or two in my time, but this one stood out at once as a prime specimen. He was tall, thin, aged and furious.

'Don't you know it's ten o'clock! What d'you want?'

'To see you for a minute, Mr. Cunningham.'

'I'm not even dressed!'

He was in a ragged dressing gown and flaming red pyjamas. There were no slippers on his long, yellow feet.

'I can wait, sir. It's very important.'

'I'm all at sixes and sevens! My housekeeper left without giving notice!'

He obviously had domestic problems; but so had I. 'It wouldn't take long, sir. I want some advice about a spiritual matter.'

He peered at me suspiciously. His hands were shaking, and his eyes had a watery tinge of red about them that reminded me of all-night drinking parties.

'If you could spare me a few minutes, sir? I can wait till you're dressed. I think we need an exorcism.'

'Exorcism, you say! Is that what you want? You can't! Not at ten o'clock in the morning!'

'It was last night. I saw this — ghost — last night.'

He closed his eyes for a moment. I knew he was trying to wish me away. Eventually he opened his eyes. He looked disappointed when he focussed on me again.

'It started with the brass-rubbing — ' I began, but that was as far as I got.

'Brass-rubbing!'

The vicar of St. James's screamed the words like a maniac.

'You want to come here and start your orgies in my church! No! In the name of St. Michael and All the Angels, no! Not whilst I can defend the church — and I can!'

I felt exhausted. Sick, exhausted and almost ready to laugh at myself. I had come for help to a raving madman.

'No more brass-rubbers in my church! Not one — no more litter-louts! None! I'll drive them from the Temple myself!'

I revised my opinion as his words penetrated my mind. I had heard rumours about this too. Brass-rubbers behaving badly were a scourge. Maybe this apparent maniac had suffered.

'I don't want to do any brass-rubbing!' I shouted, 'All I want is to know how to get rid of a ghost!'

He looked at me and tied the belt of his dressing gown tighter.

'Are you a journalist?'

'No, sir!' I calmed down. 'I'm a shopkeeper.' It sounded more respectable than artist. 'I've got a crafts shop just outside the village. In Judson's barn.'

'You're one of my parishioners, then. I suppose I'll have to listen to what you say. Now, how do you expect me to help you?'

'I took a brass-rubbing at the Stymead ruin, or rather Sally did. She's my girl.'

'At Stymead?'

He was much calmer himself now.

'Yes sir. Sally likes ruins. She found this brass under some rubble, so she took a rubbing.'

'Without permission, of course!'

'There was no one to ask. The rubbing shows a knight and his lady. And a dog. The moonlight shone on it, and it started to come to life.'

'At the church?'

'In Judson's barn.'

He was not scornful, but I could see that he was not going to be helpful.

'So you think there's a ghost in the barn?'

'Not exactly a ghost. It seems more like a real body. When the moonlight shines it takes shape.'

'How long ago?'

'Twice this week.'

'And today is?' He genuinely didn't know what day it was. A nut.

'Thursday.'

'And the date?'

'Today's the thirtieth of April.'

He didn't appear to have heard. I waited. I thought he was suffering the effects of his hangover and that he wouldn't speak to me again. But he said, eventually:

'Go away.'

'But I came for help! You should help! It's your duty!' And I remembered the fears and the terrors and the appalling miasma and the strangely ecstatic expression on Sally's face.

'My duty is to serve God.'

'Then help me!'

Cunningham looked me fully in the eyes for the first time. Eccentric he may have been: he was no madman. He knew what he was saying and doing.

'What makes you think I can help?'

'But you can! A priest can exorcise an evil spirit!'

'I can serve God, but I cannot confound His enemies, young man. The Church today is no more than a tiny island of life in a world that is raging with sin and evil. The devils are in command now.'

'But the Church could always fight the devils!'

He shook his head. 'Too many now. Too many and not enough faith. When the Church was strong, it could fight them all, all the enemies of Christ! But what can one old man do against the power of the Devil?'

'Tell me how to help myself!'

He shook his head with a tired compassion.

'You may be insane, young man, or you may have a terrible thing to face, in either case, do what I have told you to do — go away! Remember, the things of the night travel fast, but they cannot go far! So leave — leave before tonight!'

I looked back when I reached the van. Cunningham was watching me from the rotting porch, a tired old man who drank too much and could no longer fight any sort of fight.

9

I laughed a little afterwards. Partly at the antics and attitudes of the old priest, and partly at the sheer irrationality of what was happening to me and Sally.

Things like the night-beast could not happen in this day and age. They were all strictly nineteenth century stuff: they had no place in today's over-organised world. I laughed at the absurdity of it all.

I remembered that the priest hadn't laughed.

He had abused me, naturally enough if he took me for a vandal, and then he had quizzed me for a while; but he had not patronised me with a few choice verbosities about the areas of the human mind we know little of, my boy; and he had not sardonically asked if I'd been on acid. He had asked me a few fairly pertinent questions, and then he had given me some advice.

'Go away.'

He had been entirely serious. He knew of devils, and he was prepared to accept my story. As I drove the old van around without much thought of where I was going, my mind ran on his answers. After half an hour or so which anyway doesn't get you far in the High Peak, I made up my mind about the business.

I believed what I had seen and sensed. I was afflicted by some horrible phenomenon, and I thought the priest to have the right of it when he said we should get away from its haunting-grounds. We had brought it to the barn in the form of a brass-rubbing. It made sense to leave.

I did think of visiting one or other of the Priests in the Sheffield area, but decided against it. I wasn't going to leave myself open to ridicule by a pink-faced Paddy priest who would listen with half a smile and tell me to go to see a psychiatrist or lay off whatever I was hooked on.

On the other hand, I wasn't going to do nothing. I don't think I made a conscious decision to seek out the man with the pitted face, but it seemed quite natural that I should eventually wind my way through the narrow hill roads that led to Stymead. It wasn't as though I was going to see someone who was a stranger to the business. I was sure he knew a good deal about it, taciturnity notwithstanding

It was opening time when I got to the 'Black Nigget'. I saw a child's face peering out from the window of the village shop, but it was quickly withdrawn. Otherwise, I saw no one. The pub stayed resolutely locked even though I rattled the big iron latch a few times. I looked at my watch. Ten past eleven. I glanced back at the village street and again I saw a face, this time a woman's, at a window. She looked at me as if I had announced that I was the vanguard of the Martians come to first drink and then rape. Her plump red face was bright with apprehension.

I looked at my watch again. Eleven minutes past eleven. The pub should have opened at eleven prompt. Our licensing laws permit it. A light rain was falling, and the village looked more sombre than before. I looked out at the hills and saw the looming mass of a big peak I couldn't identify. Then I happened to look up at the pub's signboard.

It creaked in an iron frame, a square of painted wood. There was a grim familiarity about the picture. It wasn't the night-beast, but it was a remote and disfigured representation of it, I was sure. The head was still out of proportion. There was a suggestion of fangs, though for some reason (quite probably because that was what the last artist who had touched it up was good at) the beast had a pheasant in its mouth. *Nigget*. Yes, I thought, I know you, Nigget.

And we'll get as far as we can from you, me and Sal. And your blank-faced mistress. And this deserted village. And the bloody High Peak as well.

I turned, my curiosity blunted and my fears half-aroused again by the silence and the brooding atmosphere and the sight of the pub sign with its eerie canine figure.

A rattling of bolts behind me made me stop in my tracks.

'Is that you hammering on our door?' a

querulous whining voice demanded.

'Yes,' I said. 'Me.'

'We don't open till eleven.'

I took in the appearance of the publican. He was small and slight, thought he might have had the broad frame of a Derbyshire lead miner in his youth. He had bushy red-grey hair and a whitish complexion. No teeth. His stubble was a week old. His greasy striped flannel shirt was open at the neck, it showed a scrawny chest without any hair. I wasn't surprised to see a thick leather belt holding in place trousers several sizes too large for him. So far, the Stymead people I had met were unprepossessing types.

I looked at my watch pointedly.

'Sodding townies,' he muttered. He left the door open. I gave him a couple of minutes to open the bar. He glowered at me across the unclean mahogany counter.

'Good morning,' I said. 'I'll have a pint of shandy.'

'Bloody fancy town drinks!' He stared me in the eye. 'Bloody fancy mixtures!'

'I'll have a pint of bitter, then.'

He pulled the marble-handled pump. It must have been a local brew; I hadn't seen the name before. It was excellent.

'Will you have one?'

He pulled himself a pint of the same beer without a word of thanks. I checked my change carefully. I didn't want him to think me a complete fool. I had accepted his insults, bribed him to stop them, but I had to show him I was canny about money; there's little else to judge a man by in this part of the world. Conversation barely exists.

'I was hoping to learn a bit about the village,' I told him. 'Your pub's got an odd sign. How did it get it?'

'It was here when I came,' he said. That was all that I was going to get.

'There's some talk about the old ruin,' I tried. 'Something about it being a monastery.'

'I weren't here then.'

'No,' I said. He was being bloody-minded. I thought there was nothing for it but to plunge in. 'It's haunted, isn't it?'

'Who says?' There was some slight sign of interest.

'One of the villagers. I don't know his name. He came to my shop to tell me. He's thirtyish. Small and on the thin side. He's got a bad complexion. Acne.'

I expected a name, for landlords usually enjoy this kind of encounter, it's rather a game for them to know people by a description.

My host shook his head.

'Maybe they'd know him at the shop?'

'Doesn't open Thursdays.'

'I could ask at one of the houses.'

'You could.'

'Maybe I could find him by asking the local police.'

That didn't alarm him. 'Aye.'

He finished his beer and pointedly left me to read the racing news. I had another half of beer, which was again excellent, but I couldn't get the surly man to say anything at all now. He shook his head and grunted when I said it looked set for rain; he wouldn't commit himself about the excellence of his beer or the slack trade at the 'Black Nigget'. I found myself feeling more and more uncomfortable as I waited in the hope of speaking to one of the locals, preferably the man with the pitted face.

No one came into the pub. I was the only customer until I said, furiously, at twelve o'clock:

'What would you say if I told you the old church is haunted?'

He looked up then.

'I'd say you'd best leave it alone.'

'Gladly,' I said, recovering my temper. 'If she and her nigget would leave us alone.'

The man didn't answer. I felt a little light-headed after the drinks, and the lack of sleep; I wished to make some kind of devastatingly sardonic remark, but I have no ready wit. All I could think of was what the priest had said.

'Tonight especially,' I said to him. 'It's the end of April.'

But he didn't respond, not even by a small gesture. He didn't look up from the racing pages. When I left I knew he watched me.

Sod him too, I thought.

Sal and I were getting the hell out of the area. I have always preferred the city lights. It was only Sal's pleasure in the bleak hills that made them tolerable for me; or so I told myself then. I drove away from Stymead with the impression that my departure was marked by curtains twitching and sighs of relief and satisfaction. Another townie defeated.

The rain bucketted down as I drove out of the valley.

The hills were covered in mist, and the big black clouds swirled by, bringing with them the icy, stinging rain that could turn so easily to snow even as late as this. The windscreen wipers could hardly cope with the torrents that lashed at the van's leaky body; I felt a trickle of water down my leg. The window had rattled loose again. I began to curse with some fluency. It did no good.

I was about five miles from the barn when I saw a crossroads with a tiny shop and a red telephone box. At about the time I reached it, I remembered that we would need somewhere to sleep that night. Normally, I wouldn't have troubled to make advance arrangements. When you're nineteen or twenty, you don't. It's enough that you know you'll have a welcome somewhere, either with friends or, at a pinch, relatives. There's always someone.

However, it crossed my mind that many of the people I'd dossed with when I'd been on my own simply wouldn't be able to accommodate both Sal and myself, mainly because of the landlady problem; it's odd. Many will tolerate an extra male, but not a male with female. There was, again, the thought that Sal would be better off with someone who knew her well. So I stopped the van and rang through to her mother.

Sally's mother is a determined crusader. She's all for someone else's rights, a tireless pamphleteer, an inexhaustible addresser of meetings and charming with it; she was in the house.

'Who?' she wanted to know.

'Andy.'

'Andy?'

She pretended she'd forgotten. She had no charm to spare for me. In fact, she'd a bad case of daughter-protectionism. I went straight at it.

'I want to bring Sally over.'

'Is she leaving you?'

I sensed the hope. She wasn't campaigning for my rights. 'No! There's been a bit of trouble — I've been getting bad dreams.'

'Oh?'

I confirmed what she had always thought. A nut, that was me. Her daughter living with — not even married to — a decadent, a reactionary, a coarse, ill-bred character like me! And now I was psychotic.

'I thought it better for me to bring her over. You can put us up, can't you?'

She thought about it for some time. I could see her heavily-made-up face. She had a shrewdness that had passed her daughter by. She was wondering if Sal would get sick of me if she had to put up with my ravings in the bars.

'I'm sorry, Andy,' she said after a while. 'You see we're having a meeting of Shelter tonight in Sally's room. Any other time we'd be delighted to have you. Both of you.'

'But Sally's not been too — '

She interrupted me firmly.

'I swear by Horlicks,' she said. 'I do really. So nice to have talked with you! Get Sally to write — you'll do that for me, Andy?'

'But — '

'I have to rush! 'Bye!'

Then I rang around my own acquaintances. I had an offer from a friend of mine who's so lecherous I wouldn't entrust him with Cornelius, but I'd rung him only to find out if he would be away for the night. I turned him down. Two or three thought they might swing something with someone they knew and could they ring back, but that was no use since we weren't on the phone. It's amazing how friendships become eroded. I didn't have one genuine offer of help. I looked out at the van. We'd slept in it before but it hadn't been comfortable. With a kitten and Cornelius it'd be ridiculous.

Of course, we had money. We could go to a small hotel anywhere in the area, or outside it for that matter; but it had seemed important that Sally be with someone she knew. I found an agreeable pub a bit further on and stayed there till well after closing time eating hot pie and peas and drinking a beer that wasn't anywhere near as good as the brew at the 'Black Nigget'. When I came out of the place, it was still raining heavily and the day was as gloomy as it could be. It seemed a fitting kind of farewell for us.

I intended to make my way back to the barn, pack a few things for us and then take Sally to Manchester or Birmingham, somewhere noisy and crowded with people who could sustain a conversation for more than a couple of minutes. Sod the hills, I thought, as I drove.

It didn't work out that way. The engine faded into silence about three miles from Judson's barn. A yellow light stayed on when it should have been off. I knew enough to realise that I had bad trouble; or that the van had. In the event, it was both.

There was a garage at our small village, but it was an hour away on foot. I hadn't a raincoat with me, just the usual heavy sweater and jeans. My mildly drunken stupor didn't last long in the vicious stinging rain. I tried to hitch a lift, but no one was interested in picking up a large, bearded and stumbling yob in the half-light on a remote country road; one lorry driver slowed, but it was only to jeer at me.

'Hippie!' he bawled.

I thought of a blazing fire and a large steak; of a bottle of wine and warm sheets. We had quite a bit of money in the strong-box, which was a cracked tea-pot we kept on a shelf in the shop. Quite enough for a couple of nights of good living. After that, we'd think of something.

I plodded on. I remembered the tales I'd heard of hikers losing their way in the hills, and especially of the young Boy Scouts who had gone missing at Hag hole a year or two back; rumour had it they'd got lost down a haunted cavern, but they romance a bit in the hills. There was even talk about some kind of Devil's birthday party. I didn't laugh when I remembered the rumours; I'd seen enough in the past few nights to convince me that there was a good deal of substance in the stories from this desolate part of England.

It took me over an hour to reach the village. It was almost dark, though sunset wasn't supposed to be due for another hour.

When I got to the garage it was after five. The place was locked. I tried the house adjoining, but there was no one at home. I cursed again. With luck, we'd get a bus into Sheffield, then a train to somewhere larger where there were too many lights and too much night noise for the ghosts of the ruined church.

I turned to go to the barn. The old stone well had been dressed. Mentally I thought of the tourists the well-dressing would bring. I checked on our stocks of junk and gnomes, then I remembered we'd given up the shop. I wasn't sorry.

It had been a marvellous life for a few months, then it had turned horribly sour; with the coming of the brass-rubbing my happiness had ended. But, I told myself, I was young and strong; Sally would throw off the evil glamour of the undead thing that held her when she was far away from the gloom and mystery of the High Peak.

I determined to swallow my pride and borrow money from my parents. They're moderately well-off. A few thousand pounds would be enough to take us to Italy or Spain for the summer.

I would insist on marriage. I was old-fashioned enough to object to the way we lived together, but Sally had convinced herself that the emancipated woman didn't form a long-term contract unless it was necessary. I would assert myself. The hell with Women's Lib. All the freedom I'd give Sally in the future would be the choosing of the babies' names. I was walking ten feet high and almost growling in anticipation of my masculine dominancy when I reached the barn.

'Sally!' I bawled.

I had a premonition then. The lights were on in the shop. The living quarters were warm and cheerful. As I trailed wetly into the inner room, I heard the surviving Furry Queen yowling with excitement. It wanted to be picked up and cuddled. I wanted Sally to know who was the master of the house.

'Sally!' I bawled again.

I heard only the sullen echoes of my own voice and the anxious mewing of the unreassured kitten. Then I saw the brass-rubbing.

I fell back — I retreated two or three paces, stumbling on my bruised leg, picking myself up, and still moving away; the kitten howled now, distraught, for my fear communicated itself, as well it might.

The burned brass-rubbing was back. Neatly tacked into place it dominated the room with a cold, black insistence; the blank-faced woman had the night-beast in her slender arm. I shook with disbelief. I had seen the cylinder burn. Black smoke yellow flame, and then bright red fire; after that grey ashes. Nothing left of the loathsome ghouls that pursued us.

There was worse.

The beast at the woman's bosom showed its fangs in a savage wide-mouthed mockery of a look of affection for her. Crayoned eyes stared up at the blank face. And the terrible fangs were dappled with a horrid grue of red gore.

As I watched, I fancied I saw a rippling

154

movement of the woman's body.

'For God's sake,' I muttered, weary and sick to the depths of my soul. 'Sally, for God's sake, where are you?'

No one answered.

I knew that my desolate dream had come true. Sally had gone.

10

I looked, of course. Everywhere. But I could not go back into that room. I ran out into the night with the kitten mewing at my heels, but I returned to the shop. I forced myself to look behind stacks of paintings, in a couple of cupboards, behind the makeshift counter. I dreaded finding Sally's body — my muddled first thoughts turned on sex-killers — but I dreaded more the deep, vile forebodings that I would not give a name to,

I called to her in the darkness. I found a strong torch and shone it in ditches and amongst the dripping bushes. After a while I knew I should not find her.

I went for a coat and a dry pair of boots. I fed the kitten and comforted it too; but there was no real affection on my part, for I remembered the fate of its sister and that reminded me of Sally and the night-beast and the thing that had once been a woman. And I could feel no more than pity for the shivering hungry creature. I pushed it into its basket, where it settled, purring gently.

I grabbed some money from the cracked teapot in the shop and went out into the rain once more. *Sally! Gone? Gone?* I wanted to check up on things like her raincoat and boots, her purse, the possibility of a note saying she'd been picked up by a friend who was taking her out for a meal; but I couldn't go back into the living room. Not back to the haunted room where the thing writhed and its mistress cradled its gore-dappled head.

She was at the pub. I decided on that at once. She'd gone shopping — we had two shops in the village; then, when it was almost six o'clock, she'd decided to have a couple of gins to take away the chill of the mist and rain. I almost cried with relief. Such a simple explanation.

I ran all the way to the village pub. She wasn't there. The landlady looked a bit askance at me — I must have been quite a sight, and I spoke without much coherency. But she liked Sally, so she answered me readily enough. No, Sally hadn't been there. Had she seen anything of her? No. She wanted to know if there was anything wrong. I told her we'd had a misunderstanding about the time of her return.

'It's no night to be going far,' the landlady told me. 'There'll be a storm. There always is when the clouds come in low over the hills like this.'

I thanked her for her help, though she had given none. When I got outside again, I saw what she meant about the likelihood of a storm. Clouds were swirling thick and black over the High Peak; there was a dull-yellow gleam in the north, and through the clouds I could see a half-moon like a leopard's eye. My mind was full of barely-repressed imaginings of the worst kind. I had a half-memory of seasons and dates and the rituals of the countryside, but nothing formed clearly; the lack of food, my beer-soaked brain and the disappearance of Sally produced in me a bewildered, sad condition.

Where was she!

I rang her mother.

'Sally?' she answered sharply. 'No, she's not been home. Why should she? I said we were using her room.'

'For your homeless,' I snapped back.

'That's right! We've four problem families to house before — but what's this about Sally? Where is she? You say she's out? Andy? **Andrew**!'

I hung up on her. And still I wouldn't admit the ghastly certainty that was building up in my mind with a slow, immutable force. Not yet.

I was fool enough to call on our local policeman. His wife ushered me into a chintzy room with brass everywhere and a television set that had the smallest screen I have ever seen. He was in his shirtsleeves before a blazing coal fire. His feet were bare and red-mottled by the heat. He was called Postlethwaite.

'Here's someone to report a missing girl,' said Mrs. Postlethwaite. 'On a night like this! You look as though you could do with a cup of tea, lad. Will you have one?'

Postlethwaite reached for his socks and put them on. He told me to sit down, then he went for his notebook. I was already regretting my impulse, especially as the tea was viciously strong.

'Now, who is the missing person?' said Postlethwaite.

His broad red face wrinkled with sympathy.

'I'm not sure she's missing,' I said. 'I just dropped in to see if anyone had noticed her. She might be visiting someone — '

'Your name, sir?' said Postlethwaite. I could see the change of manner. He was fast losing sympathy with me. I could also see the tiny figures on his minuscule television set: a cops and robbers thing, with lots of guns.

'Andrew Thomas. I've got the crafts shop in Mr. Judson's barn.'

'So you have, Mr. Thomas. So you have.'

He began to tap with his pencil in the way they do when they're waiting for you to make a fool of yourself. I knew it, but I was way beyond caring if I were to appear foolish, for I could see Sally in my mind's eye as she had appeared when she had shown me the cause of all our misery — Sally, beautiful and serene in a sombre outfit, a slender figure with a mystical quality about the way she looked down at the tomb of the long-dead crusader and the wife who had now become a thing of nightmare. I could see her eyes flashing with strange lights, her lips as red as fresh blood, her whole person suddenly filled with an eerie transfiguring grace. I was very near to yelling my innermost fears.

But I didn't do. I could not bring myself to say the words. How could I tell P.C. Postlethwaite, this middle-aged utterly sane village bobby that I feared Sally had been lured away by a phantom? He had waited long enough.

'What's the missing person's name, sir?' he asked.

'Sally Fenton.'

'Age?'

'Twenty.'

He sighed.

There was a great deal in that sound. He had me placed: the queer bugger who'd turned Judson's old barn into a junk-shop. He shook his head and looked longingly at the shoot-out on the small screen.

'She lives with me!' I went on, and I

saw that I had embarrassed the man's wife sadly. 'She didn't say she was going, and no one's seen her — I don't suppose you've seen anything of her? She's about five-eight, and slim, but she's well-built — '

'I've seen the young lady before,' Postlethwaite said. 'But not today, sir.' He closed his notebook. 'Mr. Judson's been telling me he's had trouble with your dog, by the way. Reported it as a sheep-worrier. Said it's killed a lamb.'

'Cornelius wouldn't do a thing like that,' I said automatically, but my mind was far away, miles away, and remote, too, in time. I thought of that long-ago shape in its brocade, and the thing buried at the feet.

'Another two lambs killed last night, sir.'

'What?' I said, shaking my head clear. He was not able to help. I had to be on my way.

'I said Mr. Judson had more trouble with his lambs last night.' He watched me, and I thought I detected a hint of concern in his broad face.

'Is he saying Cornelius killed them?'

'He isn't, no. I'm afraid he shot your dog yesterday morning, sir.'

'What!'

'Afraid it's true, sir. Came to tell me himself, which is the right thing to do.'

Cornelius shot! I thought of his large frame, his irritating habits, and the ungrudging affection in his brown eyes; and he had been killed by the uncouth Judson. My fists came up and I looked at them for a moment. Postlethwaite shook his head.

'Shouldn't have done it, sir,' he agreed. 'He came later to tell me he'd found more lambs worried this morning. Couldn't have been your dog. Cornelius was dead by then.'

Two lambs last night, I thought. Only one the night before. The first night, a kitten's blood was enough.

'She'll have gone out, maybe, to see her folk?' suggested Mrs. Postlethwaite. 'Does happen, with a young girl.'

'I rang. She's not there.' I laughed, a bit madly. 'They need her room for a meeting of the homeless. This Shelter movement. They wouldn't let her go back tonight.'

'Still, she's of age,' pointed out Postlethwaite. 'And she's no relative of yours, sir.' He didn't add that we were living in sin, but his manner suggested it.

I didn't care what he thought.

'Look,' I said, and I spoke rapidly now. 'I went to see the local vicar this morning. He thinks there's something in it. He told me to get away, and he meant it — both of us. It all adds up! There's this blood thing which gets worse each night — I mean, they can't be satisfied with just a small quantity once they've been revived — '

'Just a minute, sir.'

' — there's been the moonlight, too. We've had three nights — you can't see the moon clearly now, but there'll be enough! It only needs a gleam or two and — '

'Sir!'

' — she didn't understand the danger! It was all interesting, even fascinating when she was awake, but in the night when the thing started to form, she was in

164

a kind of spell — '

'Stop it, will you, Mr. Thomas!'

I did. I was babbling. Postlethwaite was on his feet and his wife was bringing his boots. I laughed aloud, for I believed he had understood me at last and that he recognised the urgency of the matter.

'My van's broken down,' I said, 'so I suppose you can get a police-car sent round?'

'Won't be necessary, Mr. Thomas! A bit of a walk won't do us any harm — settle your nerves, that's what. You losing your dog and your young woman running out on you. Best thing we can do is get you back and tucked up. I'm due for a bit of a patrol, so it's no matter.'

'Walk! But Stymead's ten miles from here!'

'Stymead, lad? Who said anything about Stymead?'

I gasped in amazement. Hadn't he understood a word of what I'd been telling him? 'I did!' Then I wondered if I had, for my words had spouted and gushed into a stream of incoherent phrases. 'If I didn't, I meant to! She'll be there! At the — '

Postlethwaite was all authority now. He put a big hand on my shoulder and pushed me to the door. He shrugged into his tunic, then into an old-fashioned cape; then he set his helmet in place and he was ready to get rid of the nuisance who had stopped him from watching the real stuff on the telly.

'You're going home, lad!' he said. 'Back to the barn. Wait for the young lady there, that's what you'll do! Now, come along!'

'You don't believe she's in danger!'

'Not on your life! Lasses won't always sit waiting for lads to make up their minds! Now, come along!'

I found myself taken in a clever hold that pushed me off-balance and out into the street. Mrs. Postlethwaite called good night as if we were old friends, and I was impelled towards the barn.

'But the priest believed me! Mr. Cunningham — the Vicar of St. James's — he admitted there were devils — '

'You shouldn't go bothering Mr. Cunningham, sir! He's a few pence short of a shilling in his head! He wouldn't want to be worried — '

I interrupted him now in my desperation. I needed his help, and especially I must have a vehicle — a fast police-car for preference. More and more I was sure that I was running out of time. We passed the dressed well, with its may-branches and ribbons, its daffodils and primroses, and sprigs of yew about the arch. It would be the first of May tomorrow, but tonight there was danger, evil, there was moonlight and black clouds racing over the top of the bare hills, and I was held back by a uniformed clod who thought I was mad!

'Look, I'm not crazy! There is something loose that drinks blood — Mr. Cunningham believed me! I'm sure Sally Fenton's in danger — you've got to let me get to her!'

A distant clap of thunder shook the horizon. The rain slashed into my face. I shook myself free of Postlethwaite's restraining grip and stopped to face him. I could see indecision in his expression. He'd put me down as a madman, but there were limits. I wasn't breaking the law by my ravings, and I was making enough sense to give him a pause for thought.

'I can't stop you, lad,' he said. 'Aren't you better off waiting at home, though? It's no night for chasing about. Anyway, what's all this about Stymead?'

'That's where she's gone!'

I was full of a wild hope. I needed this slow-witted policeman's help.

'Stymead? You sure, sir?'

'Yes! She's gone to the ruined church!'

Postlethwaite tucked the strap of his helmet firmly under his chin.

'Why would she do a thing like that, sir?'

'Because she can't keep away!'

He didn't like it. There was a reluctance now in him. He wouldn't look me in the eyes.

'No, she won't be there, sir — who'd go to the old church on May Day Eve? No, forget it, sir! She's probably off to see one of her friends — had a bit of a quarrel, have you? Something you didn't want to talk about in front of Mrs. Postlethwäite? That'll be it!'

A terrible cold entered my soul. I

thought of eerie, writhing things and the terrible long fangs. Postlethwaite knew something,

'What do you mean, May Day Eve?' I asked. 'You said something about not going to the old church on May Day Eve. Tell me! Why not go to the ruin tonight?'

Postlethwaite's gaze reminded me of the way the acned man had looked at me; there was a warning and an apology in what he said, or rather in the manner of his saying it:

'Local people wouldn't go to the old ruin tonight if you gave them a pot of gold, that they wouldn't!'

'Because — '

'It's a local tale, but there's them that believe it still.'

'Well?'

'Keep away, lad! They say the boggarts roam the hills on Walpurgisnacht.'

'And at the church? At the ruin?'

'The local tale is that the dead things rise.'

I had known it, deep inside me. There had been so many hints, so many direct indications too. When I saw the figure of the night-beast I had been certain, but I had allowed Sally to laugh away my fears. Even when I saw the increasingly horrible manifestations on the next two nights, there had been strong reluctance on my part to allow a belief in the things of the night. Sally's bright eyes should have warned me, for they had contained a mesmeric light when she spoke of the undead creature that pursued her. I had been warned by the man with the pitted face and then again by the senile priest; and I had not taken heed. The things of the night had been aroused by the creeping, blazing moonlight, and they had grown stronger as they drained the life-blood from the small defenceless animals they had battened onto. Tonight they would be stronger still, for the unquiet spirits of the hills were abroad.

It was Walpurgisnacht and the diabolic legions were out. As I shivered with cold and dread, the moon swung out from behind thick black clouds. It was no longer the yellow of a leopard's eye, but bright and red as a garnet.

'You wait for a minute,' ordered

Postlethwaite. 'I'll ask if anyone's seen her.'

He went into the pub. It didn't take long. He crossed the street and gave me his news.

'Why, no worries now, sir! Miss Fenton's taken the Manchester bus three hours since. Gone on the bus, she has, all safe and sound! Mister Harris' lad Tommy saw her — her in her white boots and with a see-through umbrella, smart as paint! I bet she's gone to see someone — she'll be back right enough tomorrow, never give it another thought. I was right, lad, and I'm glad of it. Go and get some food in your belly and then go to bed!'

The Manchester bus came through our village twice a day, morning and early evening. It was a slow service, but reliable. I had used it occasionally.

'Sally gone to Manchester?' I repeated. *Why?*

I couldn't think of any reason for her to go to Manchester. It made no kind of sense. I was about to ask Postlethwaite whether she had been carrying a suitcase when I remembered the long, slow journey through the switchback valleys and around the edges of the bleak hills. I had thought of something.

The Manchester bus skirted the unholy ruined church where the undead creatures had slept for six long centuries.

'All right?' asked Postlethwaite.

'It goes to the church,' I said. 'The bus goes to Stymead.'

'Oh, that's only a coincidence!' the policeman said hastily. 'Can't mean anything! No cause for alarm, now! I can't see any need for anyone to go chasing out there — and it's not police business, not by a long chalk! You go home and get warm, lad! Off now, before we all get our death of cold!'

'*Death?*' I repeated stupidly. I saw the man's face harden. He had made his decision, which was for non-involvement. 'I have to go,' I told him. 'If I don't, the night-beasts claim her.'

Postlethwaite watched me go.

11

No one was going to help me. I knew I was entirely on my own now. It was eight o'clock by this time, and I had to get out to Stymead, which was ten or more miles away. I tried to get a taxi.

I tried six firms, but only two answered. When I said I wanted to be taken out to the village of Stymead, one man laughed at me and put the phone down. Another said he was too busy and why didn't I try the local man. He happened to be the man who ran the village garage, and I had already been there on my way to the phone booth. I couldn't get anyone to send me a hire-car either. And it all took time, precious time.

The best offer I had was that I collect a car from a company in Sheffield. It was twenty miles away.

Coins slipped through my fingers. I cursed at my ineptitude and again at the long delays as the car-hire and taxi companies failed to answer the calls. I could hardly believe it when I came to the end of the list of possibilities.

Another hour had passed. The night was wilder, I was cursing with impatience, and Sally had been gone for hours. I almost set off on foot; but I thought of the hills and the winding lanes: it would be after midnight when I reached the ruin, and that was no time to be about on the night of the demons.

I wondered if someone would lend me a car. But we had not made much friendly contact in the locality. We were on nodding and good-morning terms with a few of the villagers, but it had gone no further than that. Then I thought of Harris.

Sally had been on rather more than formally polite terms with his wife, a pleasant middle-aged woman who sold us eggs. I ran.

Fortunately they were at home. Harris himself answered my loud knocking. He thought at first I had come to see him about poor Cornelius, that I had heard wrongly about the shooting; but I stopped his explanation with a short demand for his car.

Mrs. Harris heard my hurried statements — I managed to get my story more or less understandable — and she insisted that I enter their big, flagged kitchen. Of course I didn't say anything about the night-beasts: I had learned my lesson after the Postlethwaite debacle. No one was going to trust a car to a raving lunatic.

I said that Sally and I had quarreled — it was so much more credible than the ghastly truth — and that she had set off to walk to a friend's house in a village a few miles away.

Mrs. Harris clucked and frowned, but she half-believed me. Harris was more cautious. He didn't want to become involved in a lovers' tiff, nor did he wish to release his car to someone he knew only as a new and not altogether respectable neighbour.

I was not an impressive sight, of course. Not one to inspire confidence. I was as wet as a half-drowned rat, my beard and hair ran water in streams, and my face was pale with suppressed emotion and genuine fatigue. I saw myself in a mirror and almost despaired.

Harris shook his head.

He was refusing. I tried to think of some way of convincing him without revealing the real reason for my desperate anxiety, but I could think of nothing. I was about to tell him what I had told the priest and the policeman when he said he would lend me an old motor scooter.

'It's the insurance, lad,' he told me, as I gasped in relief. 'Can't lend you one of the farm vehicles — all the cars and tractors and the like are insured as working vehicles. No one's to drive them but me and my son and the men on the farm. But there is this old scooter — you can take that if you like, because it's not strictly speaking on the books. It's one my son uses sometimes. He won't mind, won't Tommy. Not for Miss Fenton. That do you, lad?'

Harris's wife wanted me to drink tea and eat some of the leftovers from their supper, but I would have none of it. No more delays. I tried to restrain my wild impatience, and it was with extreme difficulty that I held myself back from bawling at the two kindly people as they fussed about to find gloves and a helmet. In all, it took another quarter of an hour before I had the scooter chugging through the driving rain along the road that led to the ruined church. I left with Harris's warning about taking care and his wife's call that I should bring Sally back to the farm ringing in my ears. *Back to the farm!* No! Never again to the bleak hills!

As if in answer to my angry and wild resolution to be free of the High Peak, a violent peal of thunder boomed with a tremendous explosive force around the bowl of hills in which the village stood; what had been a promise of storm became the reality. Winds gusted furiously down the valleys, pushing me from one side of the narrow road to the other, so that my progress became a crab-like motion. Lightning played in great forked tongues across the blackness of the clouds. The scooter's lamp was a tiny glow by comparison with the vividness of that vast electrical display; the sound of the small engine was lost in the thunder that followed each prolonged lightning flash. I felt numb with the successive shocks of wind, of thunder, of blue-white brilliance; and when I saw the moon, red-bright and riding the gaps in the blackness, I was close to despair, for the elements were at war with one another on this most ominous of nights, their fury a backcloth for the things that broke free of long-forgotten sepulchres: I was almost swept over a cliff-side bend in the road by one appalling blast of wind, and I cried out as I skidded on the greasy surface: what chance had I, when the night was alive with the malevolence of the night-beasts and the rioting fury of the gale?

And yet I kept on. Savage pig-headed bloody-mindedness kept me on the uncomfortable seat. I held the wet, slippery handle-grips tighter as the fury of the storm increased. I refused to be turned aside now. Too much had happened, too many terrors had scarred my mind, for failure to be considered now. I would find Sally. Find her and bring her away from the iron hills!

I pushed the small machine to its feeble limit. I doubt if I reached thirty miles an hour downhill at any time during the journey. Twice more I was near to losing myself and the machine over a steep embankment, and once I did lose control altogether as the gale blasted me into a rock face; but I remounted the still-clattering motor scooter and clenched grazed hands even more firmly about the grips.

And then I was at the church.

The weirdest effect of all was the way the ruin lay in a dead calm. After battling against the elements for maybe half an hour, I was prepared to find the tumbled stones and half-fallen walls awash with rain and scoured by the monstrous winds. It was not so.

I left the scooter at the side of the road, pushed through brambles and nettles in a gap in the dry-stone wall and half-ran, half-stumbled to the dreadful place where the night-beasts had their lair. As I neared it, I knew that the wind was no longer crashing into my face, nor was the black rain driving needles of cold pain at me. I saw a break in the black clouds and then the moon shone through with a sickly strength, a moon streaked red as a garnet stone yet producing those familiar intense beams of radiant deathly light. I might have been in a deserted and shattered amphitheatre where the floodlights still shone: in some ghostly opera house, wrecked and yet functioning in some way.

My stumbling run became an unwilling walk. I was within yards of the evil place, seconds away from the woman I loved above all else in this world. I had only to push the hawthorns aside and pick my way through the fallen stones and then I would be with her. With Sally, dressed in white. Sally of the exquisite eyes and the dreamy, sensitive face. I had reached the ruined church, my goal. All I had to do was take a few more steps.

I stopped, because I remembered the things of the night. My terrors returned, and as they did so I was aware of the intense silence in the coppice. There was no sound at all, just as there had been utter silence when we had visited the place together so few days before. It was an unsteadying, unnerving silence. And the moonlight filtered through the clouds above. Silence and moonlight, where there had been tumult and darkness. I shuddered, chilled and terrified.

I remembered Sally's strange interest in the ghastly thing that had appeared in the light. *'Isn't it weird how it all comes back to Sybil?'* she had said to me. And then, when I had fended off the apparition by making the sign of the cross, Sally had shown me how much the thing meant to her. I remembered the awed and exalted expression in her eyes.

I knew that Sally was enslaved and enamoured of the fiend of the night. And I knew that Sally had gone willingly to this frightful, deserted, haunted place. I feared what I would see.

How long I stood in the silence I couldn't say. Time seemed to hang still there. I might have been a million miles from the High Peak and its brooding, mysterious hills. Perhaps I stood there for only a moment or two, quite possibly for half-an-hour. It was the tiny sound of laughter that broke my spell.

I had heard it before, on another night of fear.

I remembered it with a shocking clearness. It was the night the thing had begun its unliving, undead existence; when the night-thing that was at its feet had crawled upward and found a horrid comfort on the bosom of the woman. My mind reeled. Was it only four days since the terrible thing had come into our lives? In the space of four days, and four frightful nights, my pleasant life had been obliterated.

Four nights!

And during one horrible night, I had heard a thin, silvery sound from the unreal lips — the lips of the woman who had been buried so many years before in the ruined church whose tumbled walls stretched to either side of me.

The ghastly creature from the grave had laughed in just such a way, but with a weaker, small sound. Now, the laughter swelled up, a high-pitched and wild noise that exulted and delighted and promised only death to whoever heard it. I knew I was listening to the evil joy of a vampire.

I walked forward.

It sounds simple. *I walked forward*. It was beyond my belief now that I acted in a sane state of mind. No. I was quite out of my mind when I walked into the place of the undead. Terror had gone. There was a grim calmness in my soul. If I must face the thing, then I must face it. *Simple?* The simplicity of doom.

I walked through the weeds and the slime of the years of rotting vegetation, and then I was in the weirdly-lit body of the ancient church. I saw a sight to overwhelm the soul.

Sally Fenton lay on the brass tablet, her arms outstretched and her eyes staring upwards and her mouth wide open, exultant, ecstatic, gasping, in a ghastly parody of sexual delight — and kneeling over her was the monster from the tomb.

The revenant had its back to me.

Even as I looked, the vampire's silvery laugh rang out and Sally joined her in that delirious sound. I heard a low, slavering noise and I saw the night-beast.

I saw blood run black in the moonlight.

Lapdog and lady, two shimmering but substantial figures, then lowered their dripping mouths to Sally Fenton's neck.

I had been prepared for this appalling scene.

The ghastly charnel-house *things* had warned me of their intent over the past four days and nights. I had experienced the stupefying miasma when the Lady Sybil and her familiar had begun to rise from the grave; I had seen her stir and become an approximation of white, living, pulsing flesh; I had heard her low gloating laughter.

Consequently, though I had no experience of the hidden, mystical sub-life of spiritualism, seances, black magic and the like, I could yet recall instinctively the ways of warding off the undead things. I had made the sign of the cross on a previous occasion, and the hazy, shimmering thing had stopped. I knew that the Cross had power.

And there was an ancient granite cross fallen from the altar long ago — I had noticed it before, on my other visit to the ruin. I knew what to do.

'*Sally!*' I yelled.

The silence was so complete that I felt time itself had died in that moonlit ruin. The revenant — the vampire from the tomb — had stopped its dreadful feeding when I called out my challenge. It did not turn.

'Sally! Sally, for God's sake, answer!'

Sally too had heard my shout. She was very still, absolutely silent. And then I saw her move her head slightly, so that she could look towards me. I saw her ashen hair in the savage moonlight like a glorious shawl about her head; and I saw her brilliant eyes, pinpoints now, but full of a strange wondering fire. Her cheeks were sunken, the bones harshly prominent; and the round column of her neck had the appearance of age.

I knew the vampire had almost drained her dry of her life's-blood. But it was more than I could do to go to her. That I could not manage, no matter how deep my love or how terrible her danger.

She had to come to me.

I staggered, half-running, towards the

wreckage of the high altar. And I called Sally to me, by all the tender names we used and by oaths I had heard as a child — biblical words full of majesty and a mysterious power. I heard myself calling on God and His Angels, and I hardly recognised my own voice; I heard too my own unnaturally high voice crying out for Sweet Jesus to save my woman and myself too, for Sweet Jesus' Sake, a heavenly messenger to come down to cast out the thing that mocked the church and all it had once been!

I believe my prayers were answered.

To this day, I hold that there was a divine intervention that night, for all the priest said about the power of the demons, I think there was enough of holiness and long-standing devoutness in the ancient church for there to be a remnant of heavenly power: for, as I yelled to Sally and made my way to the block of carven stone, the blood-red of the moon turned to orange, then yellow, then white; and the black clouds rolled across its face so that the stark whiteness was overcome and the vampire and its familiar were weakened.

It was only for moments — a few seconds.

But I realised that I might yet save Sally Fenton and, with her, my own sanity. I heard a cry from her, this time in her own voice, not that silvery, evil tone she had learned from the revenant. It was Sally, my woman, who called in the anguish of her fear.

I tried to see across the tumbled stones to the black tablet, but a mist had arisen in the body of the church. Choking, thick, grey-white and boiling with an eerie, slow motion, it was heavy with the stench of the grave. I knew fresh dangers threatened, but I could not enter that mist.

Sally Fenton must come to me.

As I waited, I felt the wet hardness of the stone. I felt a pattern beneath my fingers, and I remembered the carvings on the cross: very ancient, a thing from the days before the Normans. It showed a monster dying as a warrior speared it through and through — evil slain by a brave man. I exulted as I hefted the massive rock. *But where was Sally!*

I peered ahead, trying to make out a shape in the boiling grey-white mist. And then the clouds began to roll away from the moon, and I knew my moments of relief were passing fast.

'*Sally!*' I yelled again.

'Andy — *help me!*'

I lowered the rock. And then she called again, but I knew the voice was wrong.

'Sally, come to me!'

'Andy, you've got to come here — now!'

It was not Sally who spoke. I knew it.

'Come here!' I roared.

Then I heard the silvery laughter that jangled in my brain like an electric shock.

'Come to me, my darling! Come to me, sweetheart! Come, my heart's delight, my toad, my sweet rat, my loving nigget — come to me and let me suckle you — come to your Sally!'

And there was more, filthily lewd, words that Sally had never used, invitations that came from an utterly depraved and lost soul; and I knew it was the vampire that called.

What could I do!

I dared not, on peril of my soul, enter that filthy miasma; and yet I dared not delay, for the moonlight was filtering into the ruined church once more, bringing strength and support to the things of the night — and Sally lay in a drained torpor, not answering, and with the thing poised above her!

'Sally,' I yelled, 'if you've ever loved me, try to move away from the brass!'

It got through to her. I heard a moaning sound, and then I heard the sound of movement — plastic on rock, Sally's raincoat as it snagged on the wet stones.

The moonlight lanced down like a living thing.

As the glaring, evil light filled the church, the thick, boiling miasma receded. I saw the monster again, half in shadow, half lit by the moonlight. At its feet, the snarling night-beast that had fed it until it could seek its own frightful nourishment.

But Sally was a dozen feet away, crawling on her hands and knees towards me. Fury overwhelmed me. I saw Sally Fenton's eyes, wide and bright with shock.

I snatched up the huge broken stone that had been the cross of the ancient church. It was a ferocious effort to raise it — I am powerful, but it almost bent my back. Yet I held it high, and then I staggered forward, avoiding Sally and finally almost running as a shot-putter half-runs before he launches the missile — and I hurled the great weather-worn rock at the white figure. True and straight, the rock left my torn hands with almost a will of its own.

Sally shrieked.

Her shriek, though, was lost in the horrible, frustrated, anguished sound that came from the undead thing. I saw the shimmering flesh part and become corruption — only for moments, though, for the moonlight was pouring down to give the thing renewed force.

I waited no longer.

The cross had some mystical power of its own, for it had dismayed the night-beasts. I did not wait to see the results of my attack. I took in the first effects, saw a ghastly putrescence spurt from the exquisite shape of the thing, and then I lifted Sally and ran for the gap in the time-rotted wall.

The eldritch shrieking of the thing followed me. Another throat added to a long, vicious howling, and I knew it came from the huge-jawed familiar — I had heard the sound as it pursued the poor, lost lambs on the high fells. Lady Sybil and her familiar had been thwarted. I had freed Sally Fenton from their blood-crazed lust!

I stumbled over roots, crashed into blocks of stone, sank into mud, recovered and lurched forward again, and then I was at the lane, heart pounding, breath torn from me in harsh, racking sobs; and I heard Sally call my name. It was such a small sound, more a small animal's complaint than a grown woman's voice.

It was her own voice, though.

She was telling me she was sorry.

I felt my heart break with anguish. I forgot I had the motor scooter with me — I stumbled on through the driving stinging rain, head down and cradling her as if she were a child.

I reached Stymead as the men of that

place began to gather. They saw me and came forward. Someone took Sally from me, and I heard a quickly stifled curse.

I heard myself again, as if it were some other man speaking:

'Now will you help me!'

There was a circle of intent, resolute faces about me. No one looked away: they could meet my furious gaze.

I saw the acned man. There was a sense of fierce anger about him, and I saw that he knew what had happened.

'We know what is to be done,' he said. 'It should have been done before this.'

12

My head swam, and I pitched forward.

However, I could not let my senses leave me. I was half-held for a few moments, then I shook my head and felt the wind buffeting me, its cold clawing fingers dragging me back to full consciousness. I heard a brief argument, then I saw Sally being eased tenderly into a car. I struggled free of restraining arms and went to her just as the engine started.

'Go with her if you want, lad!' the acned man called. 'She's safe now — let him go!' he ordered.

I recognised another figure, that of the dishevelled landlord of the 'Black Nigget'. His coat shone black with rain, and his grizzled hair was plastered to his head. He was staring at me with a kind of pitying, confused anger.

'She's going to the hospital — takes quarter of an hour. Go with her.' He opened the passenger's door at the front of the car. 'In here. Come on!'

Behind me, I heard a low, fierce sound of men both afraid and determined. I looked back even as I got into the car. I saw Sally's slender shape as she lay in a coma on the wide back seat of the big old Rover. I felt the anger of the Stymead men infecting me.

They knew what they had to do, they said. I felt, intuitively, that I had to play my part in whatever desperate action they had to undertake. The acned man saw my indecision,

'Go to the hospital!' he shouted. 'See she's safe and then come back — Ben here will bring you back!'

I looked at the driver, a thickset youngish man.

'Do what they say,' the driver told me. 'Sit easy — she's in need of immediate attention, man!'

I did as I was told, with only one glance back at the rain-drenched figures of the men in the village street.

It was a wild drive, for the man at the wheel knew the urgency of the situation. He told me a little of the night's happenings at the village, but not much. He drove with a deliberate recklessness that had me gasping as we slid around tight bends awash with rain, and clung to steep hillsides by inches.

It was the landlord who had taken the initiative. He was Arthur Meggitt, and he had seen Sally when she got off the Manchester bus. The driver, Ben, told me how Meggitt had recognised Sally from the other times she had visited the church — and he had known why she went. Ben wasn't an especially articulate man, and he spoke in fragmented sentences during the whirlwind ride to the cottage hospital. He had more on his mind than the history of the de Latours family, but he recognised that I had a right to know what there was to know.

It was more than a legend. The men of Stymead had kept the records of the ancient monastery. The monks had recorded the vile and bizarre story of the Lady Sybil and her familiar and then, when the monastery was ransacked during the anti-clerical persecution of

Henry VIII's time, the old records had been preserved.

For, before the ruin was a monastery, it had been the church of the fairly important village of Stymead. And the de Latours family had been masters of the village.

It was during the time of the seventh Lord of Stymead that the terror had come. The man who was commemorated by the brass had been a crusading knight, whose taste had been for travel rather than fighting. His journeyings had taken him into countries that knew the Old Religion and kept to its ways. He had seen Styria and Croatia, and, briefly, he had ventured into the wild regions of Transylvania.

It was in the desolate mountains of this latter territory that he had found the creature. He thought he was taking an outlandish and intriguing brand of dog to his lady: it became her mentor in the ways of the Black Art, for Lady Sybil's latent evil was awakened by the nocturnal sallies of the big-jawed beast. Lady and lapdog roamed the night, learning the gorging,

insatiable and disgusting joys of vampirism.

I asked how it was that so much was
known about the time, and I had my
answer. A priest of the day, one who had
not left his name, had recognised the
things of the night for what they were. A
man of wide reading, he had learned from
his books that such things could be. The
torn animals, the staring-eyed dead children,
and the stark grey-white corpses of men
and women all over the neighbourhood of
the then-prosperous village, were the
victims of a revenant, a blood-maddened,
undying creature: a vampire.

The priest had roused the men of the
village to action. His account told how he
had instructed them in the proper
methods of confounding the power of the
night-beasts. And then the priest told how
he had come to discover the identity of
the monsters.

Indecision had paralysed the villagers.

But they had roused themselves after
the loss of three children on one night
— for the grotesque thing that inhabited
what had been the Lady Sybil de Latours

was grown impudently bold and savagely greedy. They had discovered the sleeping woman-thing and the monster that had corrupted her (and yet not, in the end, corrupted her, for the priest hinted at dark practices in her history even before her marriage to the Lord Humphrey).

'So the priest and the men of the village found them?' I asked.

We were near to the small Pennines town now. I saw streetlights and the glistening stone houses. Sally had not murmured, not once during the ride.

'Found the woman and the nigget,' said Ben. 'Found them and buried them under the brass, with white stone above to hide them. But they knew they had not finished them. The priest died that night, and all was not done in accordance with his instructions. Father to son the story's been passed down, against the day when the things should return.'

He swung the car into a narrow drive. I heard gravel crunching, and I saw the lights of the hospital.

'So the landlord knew what we'd found?'

'There's been a Meggitt in the village for nine hundred years. He knew. We all knew. We thought it was idle tradition, but we knew of the rising of the venomous serpent. Bible has it so, leastways in the old version.'

I remembered a phrase from my childhood now, just as I had remembered the words when I needed them so badly in the terrible ruined church.

' 'Protect us from the worm that dieth not',' I said.

' 'Keep us from the power of the venomous serpent',' Ben echoed, and I felt the chill of extreme horror drifting into my soul once more. I thought of the stark moonlight and the ghastly laughter; of black blood drained from the still white figure behind me.

'We finish it tomorrow,' said Ben.

He stopped the car. I flung open the door, and we took Sally Fenton inside.

We were fortunate. There was a resident night-duty staff — a sleepy young doctor and a coloured staff nurse — who snapped out of their blinking, sleepy state in a moment.

I stayed, and I asked Ben to wait with me.

We saw little but the feet of the doctor and the attendant staff as we waited outside the green plastic curtains; liquids gurgled, there was the rush of oxygen, then a quiet conversation. It didn't take long.

I got a glimpse of tubes, bottles, and Sally too, but I could not tell whether she was conscious or not. Then there were the questions.

Ben relapsed into taciturnity.

'Is there any history of anaemia?' the doctor wanted to know. He asked other questions, about excessive bleeding, about my relationship with Sally, about what she had done and where she had been. I followed Ben's lead and said little.

'The only wounds I can see are a number of small punctures in the neck,' the doctor said in a puzzled voice. 'She can hardly have been attacked in some way, can she?'

Anger brought the blood to my face, and I reeled for a moment. I thought of telling the bemused young doctor just what had happened, but I stopped myself. Now that it was over — and it was, I promised myself, for I would see the vampire destroyed before another night came! — I wanted no repercussions through the kind of publicity that would result when the popular press got hold of the story of ruins and moonlight, and night-beasts that haunted a beautiful young woman. Sally's sensitive nature would be permanently harmed if that should happen. No, I thought, let the doctor think what he might. Sally would be protected from the consequences of her seduction by the evil things.

'She'll be all right now, won't she, Doctor?' asked Ben.

'Yes, you brought her here in time. It's just a question of blood-loss. She's a common blood-group, so matching isn't difficult. But I'd like to know how she came to be in that condition.'

He looked hard at Ben and I.

'What would your guess be, Doctor?' asked Ben.

He shrugged.

'I've never seen a case like it. What kind

of creature do we have in this country that can cause this kind of blood-loss? It can't be. I'll check her medical history as soon as it's decently daylight. Give me the name of her G.P.'

I provided the necessary information, and then I settled to a long wait. I had promised myself at least another couple of hours at the hospital. I would wait until she knew me; until I had satisfied myself that she was free of the revenant.

Ben waited with a barely-concealed impatience. Two o'clock came, then the minutes slowly ticked away on the hospital clock until it was three o'clock. We drank tea, a kindly orderly kept us supplied, and Ben completed his story of the legend of the Stymead church and its loathsome vampires.

The unfortunate victims of the fourteenth-century outbreak of vampirism had to be taken from the graves. This much was done in accordance with the priest's instructions, for any one of the corpses, be it that of man, woman, or child, might have become, in turn, a night-creature. Each was exhumed and subject to the terrible butchery ordained for the destruction of a vampire.

It was all in the ancient records. The plague had been stopped before it could destroy the whole village. And yet the village had declined in population as well as importance. The baleful effect of the haunting had not altogether faded, even now. Stymead became a sad, lost village, sparsely-settled, and not a place where strangers felt welcome. Those that came with the intention of settling did not stay long.

'We brought the thing back to life,' I said.

'It was accidental,' Ben told me. 'You had no way of knowing.'

'Yet we did it. It was the moonlight.'

So I told him about the nights of terror.

'The moonlight on the pictures,' Ben said wonderingly. 'There was always a fear of moonlight in the village — we knew the Lady Sybil would be strong if the light of the moon fell on her, especially on a devil's night like this. May Day Eve. But moonlight on her picture!'

'When Sally saw her, she couldn't keep away from her.'

Ben nodded.

'It was told that way in the legend. The vampire fixes on one person and won't keep away from whoever it chooses. They say the one it finds becomes enamoured, like a kind of love, until all its life is sucked away.'

I shivered now. The night was passing, and there was work to be done. I got to my feet and sought the night-nurse.

She agreed that Sally was sleeping peacefully, and she checked with the doctor to see if I might go to look at her.

Against the white of the sheets, she was thin-faced and frail-looking. But the grey-whiteness of her skin had gone. The corpse-like appearance and texture of her marvellous complexion had changed into a semblance of living colour. Though her naturally pale skin was paler than usual, I could see that the vital transfusion had brought life to her cheeks. A pulse beat steadily in her neck.

'Sally?' I whispered.

The nurse pushed me back with a warning murmur.

'She has to sleep. She was in shock

when she came — she's fast asleep now, so try not to speak.'

'I only — '

'Leave her with us. She's safe now.'

I looked at the big, motherly woman and thought of the ghastly thing that had knelt beside Sally so short a time before; I felt myself gaining confidence. This was a place of safety. The nurse was right.

I saw Sally smile a little in her sleep, as though she could hear what we were saying. I felt a rush of affection for her — I could have lifted her from the bed and hugged life and strength into her, tired and demoralised as I was. Tomorrow would be soon enough to speak to her, I decided.

When the night-beasts were utterly rooted out and Stymead at last free of their evil spell.

I looked again from the doorway of the room. The lights were low. Ben was waiting for me, trying to conceal his urgent desire to be on his way.

Then I saw Sally smile again.

It puzzled me that smile, for it was like something I had seen before; and something I didn't want to admit to seeing. There was a hint of knowingness about it that set my mind veering into uneasy byways. Just then the night-nurse dimmed the lights further, and I put Sally's smile down to a trick of shadow.

She had been turning slightly in her sleep, I decided. There had been just the one small affectionate smile when we were talking, the night-nurse and I; no other.

'Fit?' asked Ben. 'Daylight in two hours.'

'I'm ready. I know what's to be done.'

'But can you do it?'

'Who else?'

13

We drove back as quickly as we had come. The night was less wild on the return trip. I couldn't feel the power of the gale so strongly. Even the ton-and-a-quarter of the big old car had been pushed about on the winding roads during the journey to the hospital; but the elements now were subsiding. Rain drilled at the windscreen, but not so fiercely. A few blue-white streaks of lightning illuminated the High Peak, but not with the dazzling intensity of a few hours before. And the darkness was fading.

When we reached the village, Ben kept on. I knew where we were heading. I was vigorous again, for hate burned in me like a fire — hate blotted out all thought of Sally Fenton, all I lived for was the gory task that must be mine.

When I look back now on the night of the demons, I find myself consumed with a grieving and bitter anger at myself. I ask how I could have been so blind. But I know, in my innermost heart, that it was the primitive and little-understood parts of the mind that are normally kept in check, which drove me on in so unthinking and unconsidering a way. I was a savage, committed to a bloody and savage ritual.

I forgot the power of the enemy. I, who had seen the ghostly manifestation in the stark moonlight. I, who had seen flesh formed from nothing more substantial than the haze-motes coruscating in the whiteness. Yes, it was I who forgot, who miscalculated, who brought the bitterest doom — but I go on too far. It was hidden from me for a while yet.

When we reached the church, I thought it was almost over. I knew there would certainly be a horrific encounter: what passed later was mercifully concealed in the mists of the future. For the time being, I was almost happy. I exulted in my strength, and I felt a surging pride in my achievements. I had saved Sally Fenton from the vampire, and now I would destroy it.

Dawn was near as we entered the ancient ruin.

The sight that met my eyes broke my dream.

I have said earlier that I dreamt an appalling dream of loss and life-long despair — it was the night when the nigget, Lady Sybil's familiar, began its evil hauntings — and I recalled now its peculiar horror.

In the dream I saw a mound of soil, a ring of angry faces — and an open grave.

I felt myself gasping for breath, for the men of the dream were before me now. So was the heaped mound of soil. And the open grave. Within it, I glimpsed red-rusted iron armour and rotted bone.

All that was missing was the white-shrouded form I had seen in my dream. Cold tendrils of fear began to drift through my mind; terror was not far away.

I saw the landlord of the 'Black Nigget' staring at me from red-rimmed eyes. His hands were stained with mud. The other men of Stymead showed the same signs of having laboured in the night. Now, they waked. In the light of their lamps I saw tools stacked.

I pushed my fears aside as I stood at the edge of the open grave. I was one of that quiet circle.

'She'll return?' I asked.

Meggitt, the landlord, nodded.

'No other earth will hold her. She has to come back to this place when the first light comes over the hills.'

I felt a tremor of doubt.

'What if she doesn't come?'

'She will,' said the acned man. 'She has to hide from sunlight, and she knows only this soil. She's lain here for hundreds of years, and she's lost her cunning. She won't know how to hide, except here.'

I saw the brass tablet, now secured and bent.

'It was the moonlight — ' I started to say.

'Aye,' said Meggitt. 'But you did well afterwards. There's no blame in it for you.'

'I threw the old cross at her — '

'We guessed,' said the acned man. He seemed worried too. In the pre-dawn light

I saw that he and the others were grey-faced; it was not just the fatigue of the night's exertions that had brought them to this state. They knew the revenant was near.

'I must have smashed the brass,' I went on. 'I wish to God I'd never seen it!'

We all felt the biting cold at the same time.

There was only the smell of the moist earth, the sharp light of the lanterns, and the dampness of the Pennines early morning: and then the cold struck.

I had known it before.

The grey-white miasma came with the cold.

Indecision gripped the men. I saw their faces through the bitter, nauseating mist, and I knew they might break and run and all our preparations would be for nothing. Beside me, Ben trembled violently.

The frightful grave-stench made me retch. I held down the bile. My fists clenched till I felt the flesh tear. Courage wasn't enough. My companions were at the further extremity of fear. One man sighed and began to slide to the ground.

The acned man rallied them.

'She can't harm us! We've the garlic and the old cross here — keep to your places and stand still!'

'Aye,' growled Meggitt. 'It's to be done right this time — done to the death!'

'See!' whispered Ben.

I had not yet seen the face of the thing. The miasma seemed to become solid. In the midst of the grey-white, swirling fog, I discerned a shape that had the eerie elegance of the manifestation I had seen at the barn. At its feet was a long-bodied snuffling thing. Both figures were shadowy, but both had the firmness of living beings.

'God!' muttered Meggitt.

I saw what he had noticed.

As the fearful mist progressed across the tumbled stones in the chancel, a trail of red-black liquid remained to mark their passing. Spots of blood lay on the wet stone, drippings from the jaws of the night-beasts.

Another tremor of apprehension shook me. The things had fed well. They moved with slow steps, as if gorged to repletion

212

and ready for the long day's sleep. I saw the firmness of the vampire's flesh when a hand came into view; the sight brought a drawn-out murmur of incredulity from the men. They had believed the story handed down from their ancestors. They had believed me when I told of the coming of the vampire. This was something again.

To see the thing in the flesh was different.

Across the centuries, the Lady Sybil de Latours reached out to become firm-bodied, vital, a creature of apparently living flesh. The grey-white column hid her once more. I think it was her protection now that the moon was no more than a white stone in the sky and the clouds were tinged with the first signs of dawn.

She did not seem to notice us.

I thought I heard a small, harsh sound from the smaller, ground-hugging shape of the familiar at her heels, but I might have been mistaken. The night-beasts were tired, satiated with blood. They wanted the wetness of the earth about them and the dank stench of rotted winding-cloths in their nostrils. After a long night's fleeting, shadowy, swift-moving feasting, they longed for the grave's protection.

They hesitated at the edge of the gaping pit.

I wondered if Lady Sybil knew that the bones of her lord and master, the crusader Lord Humphrey, had been disturbed and his rusty armour disarrayed. If so, it seemed to cause her no concern.

I saw the miasma fall away and, just as the first rays of weak sunlight hit the remains of the tower, I looked fully at the Lady Sybil.

What a woman she had been!

Undead, blood-crazed, monstrous thing from the tomb she might be but there was no doubting her beauty. Deep eyes, eyes like dark pools, shone in a dead-white face. Her features were sharp and regular, with high cheekbones and a thin aristocratic nose. There was a glamorous air about her, as if she knew we watched and waited in awe at her majestic beauty. And all this exquisiteness was for nothing. The flawless skin was dabbled with gore, the well-shaped chin partly obscured by red-black blood. So much beauty, and, with it, the curse of vampirism.

She smiled down into the wet pit that was her couch. The lapdog nuzzled her bare feet. When she opened her lips in that smile, I remembered with a sick premonition that Sally had smiled too.

I forgot Sally when I saw the pointed teeth in the blood-bright mouth. White teeth glistened, the slender and sharp fangs of the vampire. And then the creature subsided into the grave.

Oblivious of us, she seemed to fade into nothingness in the weak sunlight. One moment she stood by the open pit, and the next she was gone. For a second or two I thought I saw an outline of the vampire and her familiar, but only momentarily.

I sighed, a sigh that was echoed in the expelling of air by the frightened men around me.

Arthur Meggitt looked towards me. Sweat stood coldly on his lined face. Yet there was no weakening of the resolution I had seen in him during the night hours. He took a bottle of whisky from his pocket.

'You'll need this,' he told me.

'And this,' said the acned man.

I drank as much as I could. The whisky brought a spasm of coughing, but it kept down the vomit that had been threatening to rise up.

Then I took the heavy-bladed knife from the other.

I had seen its gleaming, square blade in the light of the men's torches. I hadn't realised how heavy it would be. I held the handle and saw the thickness of the steel.

It was a butcher's knife.

The men waited for me to say something, but I could think of nothing appropriate. The acned man seemed to think I needed an explanation.

'We were going to ask a priest to come, but we decided against it,' he told me. 'I tried to warn you when I came out to your shop, though I knew it was probably too late. Can you do it?'

'Yes.'

'Strike firm,' said Meggitt. 'More whisky?'

'No.'

The bottle was passed around, and then the men took off their dripping coats. I hardly noticed that the rain was gone. Sunshine filtered through the low cloud. The silence in the ruin was overpowering.

'We dug the pit deep enough and wide enough to give us room to work,' said Meggitt. 'Ready?'

'Don't look into her eyes,' warned the acned man.

'No.'

'First her, then the dog. Through the neck. One blow. You're strong enough.'

I was. None of the men assembled in an angry, fearful ring about the pit could have been called well-built, let alone powerful, apart, that is, from Ben. And his twitching face and trembling hands disqualified him from the task they thought mine.

We lowered ourselves down into the great pit. Stones crunched under my heel. Then someone passed down a spade, and they left it to me to scoop away the light covering of earth that hid the body of the long-dead but eerily undying Lady Sybil de Latours.

Meggitt took hold of the rotting winding-sheet. It came away with a sucking noise. And we saw her.

Lady Sybil. Her familiar.

Both lying and breathing in the grave.

Blood clung to their lips. Blood on her bright ruby lips, blood on the jaws of the monster at her feet. If she had opened her eyes, we would have trampled one another down in a mad, terrified rush for safety. I think I would have killed the man that got in my way.

Meggitt acted swiftly.

He knew the sickening power of the monster. In the daylight, she was nothing but a sleeping figure; but, even in the daylight, she could look one in the eye and cause such acute feelings of horror that we should have been unmanned.

Meggitt whispered fiercely.

One of the men passed down the stake. Ash, I saw. Good strong ash, with the point as sharp as a spear.

I looked down at the slender, elegant form. She was clad in the dress from the brass-rubbing. Time had not affected the rich brocade. Reds and greens, and glinting gold, showed in its folds. Meggitt poised the pointed stake over her slack bosom.

I hefted the knife.

'One blow!' warned the acned man savagely.

'God help us,' I breathed.

The monster at her feet gave a sullen growl, as it dreamt of the dangers nearby. It did not move, however.

'Strike!'

I heard the Derbyshire man's voice and aimed for the soft neck.

She opened her eyes as the blade bit and passed through flesh, muscle, tendons and bone. Her eyes came open and I saw a flashing, wild rage, a demon's basilisk stare, the fires of hell in those haunted pits of eyes. As her head flew free into the wet mud, a piercing shriek rang out in the pit, to be echoed and re-echoed, so that the ancient church was filled with the pain and grief and rage of the dying Lady Sybil.

Immediately the knife came down, Meggitt plunged the stake into her evil heart. Blood, a venomous black blood, made a fountain in the grave. It spurted and splashed for a few moments, then slackened.

As the noisome fountain diminished, I struck off the head of the familiar. It opened wide jaws, and I saw its vampire teeth, needle-sharp, long and dreadful. Then Meggitt took another stake and pinned its writhing body to the ground.

I heard the men growl in answer to the small beasts threatening and dying snarls. I looked up and saw their faces. They were flushed and feverish. The reign of the monster was over.

Even as I stood over the corpse of the woman, with her blood on my boots, I saw the white flesh shrivel. The arms became withered, yellowing and then turning black. The flesh crumbled into a horrid detritus, then it flaked away into the mud, leaving white bone which turned black in moments. The skull, which had been so beautifully fleshed with the vampire's exquisite features, grinned briefly, white bone and white teeth; then it too acquired the aspect of extreme age, decaying and joining the crumbling bones of what had been the corpse of Humphrey de Latours, Lord of Stymead.

The artist's intention was complete. At last the remains of the Lord and Lady of Stymead were together and would remain so until the day of the resurrection.

I wondered if the men of Stymead would replace the brass over the poor remains. It didn't seem to matter.

A great weariness came over me.

I looked down at my hands. Black mud, and the creature's blood, made a grim sight. Meggitt, I saw, was looking down at his own hands with an expression of awe on his face.

The acned man summed up what we thought

'It had to be done,' he said quietly. 'And now it is done, God have mercy upon her soul. We'll cover them up and be done with it.'

14

The rest of my tale is soon told. I cannot dwell long on the details, indeed much of what happened is now only a blur. Too much came too quickly. The creatures that roam the night are too fast for ordinary men. They strike as we collect our scattered thoughts, throwing us into a bemused stupefaction.

The night-beasts are deadly fast.

I went back to the barn. I insisted on riding the motor scooter, despite Meggit's offer of a car-ride. I don't know why I refused. Perhaps I felt I should return Harris's clattering vehicle as soon as possible, in view of his kindness.

The kitten had been fed. Harris's wife, I thought. I patted it absently and thought of sleep. Then I realised I was ravenously hungry, so I tore off my wet coat and went into our living room.

I saw the ridiculously elaborate French bed and a brief memory of happy times came to me; behind me, the kitten set up a sound much like a wail of fear.

I heard my own hoarse bellow of amazed, incredulous, stunned gasping terror.

'No! *No!* For God's sake, *No!*'

I stood yelling incoherently for minutes, then Harris happened to pass and heard. He saw me and went for Postlethwaite.

I was still bawling at the top of my voice when the two men pulled me away from the dreadful wall.

'Man, what is it?' demanded the policeman. 'Control yourself — Thomas, come away!'

I heard him tell Harris something about my being an unbalanced and superstitious young fellow who'd come the night before with some tale about a girl and a ruined church.

Harris talked back, the two men's voices merging into my own words now, for I could speak to them.

I pointed to the brass-rubbing.

'Look!'

They looked.

Postlethwaite's red face drained.

'By God!' he murmured.

Harris recognised the face too.

'It's just like — '

I felt myself collapsing. They held me by the shoulders.

'Last night there was no face there,' I said in a resigned voice, for I knew what I should hear soon. 'Now it's Sally Fenton.'

Harris shook his head.

'Lad, I don't know what's happening, but there's something here that calls for an explanation.'

'No,' I said. 'I know why she's there.'

'Come to the farm,' said Harris.

'No. I've something else to do.'

'Later, lad!' Harris said.

'Now. I'm grateful, but I've got to go to Sally at the hospital.'

'Hospital?' said Postlethwaite. 'Is she ill? Has she had an accident?'

'She's dead. And it wasn't an accident.'

'What!' roared Harris. I think he suspected me for a moment. After all, I had the look of a murderer on the run. I was haggard, my clothes were stained and torn, and I had the monster's black blood on my boots.

Postlethwaite became official.

'When did this happen, sir?'

'Some time this morning. Just before dawn.'

'You were at the hospital, sir?'

'No. At Stymead.'

Postlethwaite passed a hand over his brow. 'So you went there, sir?'

I told them I had found Sally and that she had been taken immediately to the cottage hospital.

'So you left her, sir. Then what?'

I knew I could not tell him the rest. I had a duty to the men of Stymead. They had tried. Tried their best, in the face of a ravening night-beast. That they had failed to save Sally was not their fault.

I felt quite calm then. I knew I could face the decision ahead of me with equanimity. I looked again at Sally's face. She looked back with a tender tranquillity from the now-stained and battered brass-rubbing.

She was at peace.

Not for long, though. She would sleep

in the daylight hours.

'I'd like to go to the hospital,' I said.

'I'll take you,' said Harris.

'I think I'll come along,' said Postleth-waite. 'In view of the circumstances.'

'In view of the circumstances,' I agreed. It didn't matter what they said. I was very calm. Despair can be a peaceful state. You don't fight against the inevitable.

They were very sympathetic. I lacked only the details, and these were forthcoming readily.

A lady had visited Sally during the night. She had introduced herself as a relative, and she had at once agreed that she was Sally's mother. There was a family likeness, I could see that now.

I remembered vaguely what I had heard of the remarkable persistence of the vampire. They will not give up once they become attracted to a particular victim. Their cunning is limitless.

And the undead travel fast, very fast.

The night-nurse had not allowed the lapdog to go into the ward. And when the tall, elegant lady in the rather old-fashioned dress had looked at the sleeping figure, Sally had at once awakened.

The nurse suspected nothing.

There was the kind of glad greeting between the sweet-smiling revenant and Sally that one would expect from a loving older woman and a girl of Sally's years.

No one watched.

No one saw the vampire leave. They leave no trace of their passing.

And, whilst we had waited around the monster's grave, she had drained the life-blood from Sally Fenton.

There was a savage irony about it that almost amused me. I could happily have abandoned myself to the roaring laughter of insanity had it not been for the one last duty I must perform.

Postlethwaite made inquiries.

No possible blame could attach to me, though there would have to be an investigation. Meanwhile, I was advised to remain in the neighbourhood and leave a note of any change of address with the police.

Harris invited me to stay at the farm for a few days. I refused. I left the hospital and went back to the barn.

Harris dropped me off with a warning. It was to the effect that I should not sit brooding for long, that I was a young man with talent who had a way to make in the world. He said he'd send his wife with some supper, and I thanked him.

I slept a little.

Sally's mother stormed into the living room where I lay — I had no fear of the sweet face in the brass-rubbing, for fear was quite gone now — and she cursed me with a virulence and an abandoned obscenity that shocked me. I let her have her say. Her father clasped and unclasped his hands nervously. I told them I thought Sally had suffered some kind of seizure and left it at that.

Eventually, Mrs. Fenton was exhausted and her husband led her away.

Again I slept, this time uninterruptedly.

It was dark when I awoke. I looked out of the high window and saw thin cloud over the peaks. It was too early yet for the moonlight.

Mrs. Harris had left a meal. It was an excellent cheese pie; there was a bottle of beer with it. I thanked her silently for her tact in not arousing me.

When I had eaten, I washed myself and put on a clean shirt. I don't know why. Or perhaps I do. It's no compliment to a woman to meet her in a dishevelled and dirty condition.

I looked through Sally's things. I wasn't at all surprised to find her notes. She'd told me she had done some research on the Stymead ruin. I read her fine-flowing artist's hand without any sense of loss as I was reading. I nodded when I had finished.

She had traced her own family tree. A distant ancestor was a de Latours.

I found myself smiling now. Everything was in place. Sally rested — for a while.

I lay on the bed and watched the brass-rubbing as it slowly became luminescent. The moonlight was thin and weak at first.

Then it strengthened.

I felt almost happy. Despairing, of course, but curiously happy. My youth was at an end. Perhaps my life too.

Would I welcome her when she came?

That she would come to me I did not

doubt. Those that die of the vampire's terrible embrace become, in turn themselves creatures of the night.

Sally would rise from the cold mortuary slab.

The moonlight now suffusing the black and white of her exquisite face and delicately-proportioned figure would bring her to a new and delicious existence.

And what would I do?

I thought of the ring of bitter, aggrieved faces. I thought of the vast open pit. I shuddered when I recalled the basilisk's terrible stare as the head sprang from the white column of the neck.

How could I turn Sally Fenton over to the men of Stymead?

I smiled again now, and, as if in answer, I saw the corners of Sally's mouth twitch up. There was a sudden flooding of bright white moonlight, and I became fiercely excited.

I waited for my love.

Other titles in the
Linford Mystery Library:

THE FROZEN LIMIT

John Russell Fearn

Defying the edict of the Medical Council, Dr. Robert Cranston, helped by Dr. Campbell, carries out an unauthorised medical experiment with a 'deep freeze' system of suspended animation. The volunteer is Claire Baxter, an attractive film stunt-girl. But when Claire undergoes deep freeze unconsciousness, the two doctors discover that they cannot restore the girl. She is barely alive. Despite every endeavour to revive the girl, nothing happens, and Cranston and Campbell find themselves charged with murder . . .

THE SECRET POLICEMAN

Rafe McGregor

When a superintendent in the Security Branch is murdered, top detective Jack Forrester is assigned to the case. Realising his new colleagues are keeping vital information from him, Jack Forrester sets out to catch the killer on his own. But Forrester soon becomes ensnared in a web of drug traffickers, Moslem vigilantes, and international terrorists. As he delves deeper into the superintendent's past, he realises he must make an arrest quickly — before he becomes the next police casualty . . .

THE SPACE-BORN

E. C. Tubb

Jay West was a killer — he had to be. No human kindness could swerve him from duty, because the ironclad law of the Space Ship was that no one — *no one* — ever must live past forty! But how could he fulfil his next assignment — the murder of his sweetheart's father? Yet, how could he *not* do it? The old had to make way for the new generations. There was no air, no food, and no room for the old . . .